MISSING PERSONS, ANIMALS, AND ARTISTS

MISSING PERSONS, ANIMALS, AND ARTISTS

ROBERTO RANSOM

TRANSLATED BY DANIEL SHAPIRO

SWAN
ISLE
PRESS

Roberto Ransom (b. 1960, Mexico City) is an award-winning narrative writer whose published work includes novels and collections of short stories, poetry, and essays as well as children's literature. In addition to *Missing Persons, Animals, and Artists*, Ransom is the author of two other short-story collections, *Saludos a la familia*, and *Vidas colapsadas*; the novels *En esa otra tierra*, *La línea de agua*, *Te guardaré la espalda*, and *Los días sin Bárbara*; and the novella *Historia de dos leones* published as *A Tale of Two Lions* (W. W. Norton, 2007). He is a tenured professor in the School of Fine Arts and School of Humanities at the Autonomous University of Chihuahua.

Daniel Shapiro is the author of three poetry collections, most recently, *Woman at the Cusp of Twilight*, as well as a translator of Latin American literature; his translation of Tomás Harris's *Cipango* received a starred review in *Library Journal*. He is a distinguished lecturer and editor-in-chief of *Review: Literature and Arts of the Americas* at The City College of New York, CUNY.

Swan Isle Press, Chicago 60628

Edition©2017 by Swan Isle Press
©2017 by Roberto Ransom
Translation©2017 by Daniel Shapiro
All rights reserved. Published 2017

Printed in the United States of America
First Edition

20 21 19 18 17   12345
ISBN-13: 9780997228717 (paperback)

The following stories have appeared in these publications:

Electric Literature (no. 4, Summer 2010)
 "Three Figures and a Dog"

The Quarterly Conversation (issue 21, September 2010)
 "Lizard à la Heart"

Mandorla: New Writing from the Americas (no. 15, 2012)
 "Viola di Bordone" and "Vasari, Do You Hear Me?"

Library of Congress Cataloging-in-Publication Data

Names: Ransom, Roberto, 1960- author. | Shapiro, Daniel, 1955- translator.
Title: Missing persons, animals, and artists / Roberto Ransom ; translated by Daniel Shapiro.
Description: First edition. | Chicago : Swan Isle Press, 2017. | Originally published in Spanish under the title Desaparecidos, animales y artistas (México, D.F. : Consejo Nacional para la Cultura y las Artes, 1999).
Identifiers: LCCN 2017015759 | ISBN 9780997228717 (paperback)
Subjects: LCSH: Ransom, Roberto, 1960---Translations into English. | Mexico--Fiction. | BISAC: FICTION / Short Stories (single author).
Classification: LCC PQ7298.28.A447 .A2 2017 | DDC 863/.64--dc23
LC record available at https://lccn.loc.gov/2017015759

Swan Isle Press gratefully acknowledges that this book has been made possible, in part, with the generous support of the following donors:

FRANCIS HIGGINS

EUROPE BAY GIVING TRUST

The paper used in this publication meets the minimum requirements of the American National Standard for Information Sciences—Permanence of Paper for Printed Library Materials. ANSI/NISO Z39.48-1992.

To my father and mother

To Rosa María

Acknowledgments

Missing Persons, Animals, and Artists is more than contingent, and the fact it exists at all is thanks to dear friends who so desired it: Álvaro Uribe, the editor of the original *Desapareci-dos, Animales y Artistas,* and his wife, Tedi López Mills, also a dear friend who goes way back; Dan Shapiro, my translator to English and tireless promoter of this book; Thomas Colchie, my agent for a few years; Tom Mayer, the editor of my previous work in English and staunch supporter of my work; and David Rade, my present editor; all of them very dear friends, excellent craftsmen, brothers in another culture and language who have shown great care for this book. My gratitude also to Marianne Jankowski, the bold and enthusiastic designer of *MP, A, & A.* I must mention that I have not met in person several of these friends, which just goes to show one of the virtues of the nature of writing, and the bonding and embodied nature of voice. Joby and Beth Taylor, and Larry and Peggy Bouchard, and M.sP. José Torres Rojas have been fellow travelers on this stretch of the road–albeit all at a physical distance. Of course, foremost, my dear wife and children, my first readers and critics, who have participated in every step of this project with their loving sup-port and lucid observations. All of the above would be lacking if I didn't mention that this shared work, over many years, has been a cause of joy, laughter, and meaning in my own life, for which I am deeply grateful.

Contents

Illustrations

The following are credits for images that appear on the cover and interior of *Missing Persons, Animals, and Artists*:

Frontispiece: Plaza de Armas de México/C. Castro del. y Lito.

Lizard/by ilbusca, used under license from iStock.com.

Frog/ by ilbusca, used under license from iStock.com.

Detective/ by 4x6, used under license from iStock.com.

Silouhette of Woman/by Oksanita, used under license from iStock.com.

Crocodile/by THEPALMER, used under license from iStock.com.

Anguis Fragilis (snake)/by ilbusca, used under license from iStock.com.

Dog (Hungarian Vizsla)/by antiqueimgnet, used under license from iStock.com.

Chanterelle/by Epine-art, used under license from iStock.com.

Cherub/by nicoolay, used under license from iStock.com.

19th century color engraving of bull/by antiqueimgnet, used under license from iStock.com.

***

Child's hand holding brush/by moopsi, used under license from Shutterstock.com.

Brown paper texture/by homydesign, used under license from Shutterstock.com.

Antique pocket watch/by MoreVector, used under license from Shutterstock.com.

Cross drawing/by Channarong Pherngjanda, used under license from Shutterstock.com.

Violin/by MoreVector, used under license from Shutterstock.com.

I can psoakoonaloose myself any time I want.

—JAMES JOYCE, *FINNEGANS WAKE*

MISSING PERSONS, ANIMALS, AND ARTISTS

Lizard à la Heart

to the Tuesday friends

*This fantastic animal was usually referred to as the
"cruell craftie crocodile."*
—JEAN-PIERRE HALLET

Tears, idle tears, I know not what they mean.
—TENNYSON

The bathroom hasn't been open for days. Under the door, as
always, it smells like a swamp. The last time I opened it was
to throw you two dead chickens: I know that when you're very
hungry, you'll accept cadavers. The bathroom is another world
that's been transforming from a typical space in houses of this
development, located on the second floor along with the bedrooms, shared by the whole family, to *your* place, which is neither terrarium nor aquarium but both things. The shower has
been turned into a bathtub, the tile floor has been covered with
gravel and sand, the little window has been enlarged to let in
more light. The changes didn't happen right away. We claimed

1

we were doing it for ourselves. We'd always wanted a bathtub in a spacious bathroom filled with light.

The neighbors have gotten tired of complaining. They know that House 17 smells bad. They like their musk in perfume. You no longer feel offended when I tell you that. Personally, I like your smell, it makes me giddy. Sometimes they hear blows against the wall, as if from a very heavy object. The house is closed to everyone outside. They don't know that it's your tail, which you learned to wag, imitating the dog in the house. Then, as could be expected, without a model or playmate, you forgot why tails are wagged—you do it with your whole body—and now, above all, you choose moments of rage or frustration. You want to knock down the walls. The house-paint is peeling, no one has cut the grass, the doorbell doesn't work. Number 17 lowers the value of the neighborhood. They think I'm a widow accompanied by a dog that sometimes howls at night. They think you're a dog, can you imagine? An enormous dog sniffing the underwater lamp-posts. The house is a magnet for children; they dare each other to see who can penetrate further from the street into what looks like a vacant lot. They walk through the tall grass as if they were swimming, leaving a wake behind them. Among the bushes and under stones, they find snakes that they toss in their pockets. There are also field-mice and lizards. They hunt them with slingshots and B.B. guns. But they've stopped coming since they broke one of the front windows and there was no reaction from either the *señora* or her dog. That scared them a little and after a while, eliminated any risk of—and therefore their interest in—vandalizing.

I don't have to open the door to know that right now you're crying. Your smell attracts me. I feel affection for you. You know that, but I shouldn't come in. I'll sit here, next to the door, so you can talk to me. I'm also lonely but so what? You're not going to solve anything by hitting your tail against the wall. You're no longer a baby. Ay, it's no longer possible to carry you in a plastic bag!

I used to go with my son to the pet shop near the Saturday Bazaar, alongside Batallón de San Patricio Park. Miguel liked you. I asked him, why not a canary? They're related, you know. Most of your relatives became extinct 120 million years ago. Nevertheless, just recently, you'd cracked your eggshell open with a beak; and then you made short, sharp barks like a Pekinese. You were incubated in that dark, dusty place, among collections of moths pinned to the walls. The owner was a collector. His fondness for reptiles was obvious. He also had a section of exotic animals and that's where we found you. You were from the Nile. I found you attractive. You were so small and grotesque. Like a fat, lazy lizard. You looked nightmarish. It didn't make sense that they'd be putting you in a plastic bag like the ones I used to wrap my son's sandwiches and, what's more, immerse you in water. There was nothing fishlike about you. You sank to the bottom as if a bit surprised, rose again, floated, glanced outside, but . . . above all you paddled with your stubby feet and moved vertically through the water and this added to your charm because you looked like a little seahorse. We bought you an aquarium, with colored marbles lining the bottom.

It's not true that I wanted to kill you. Simply put, when you grew long enough to touch the glass walls, on one side with your snout and the other with your tail, I thought there was no reason to order a larger aquarium, or should I say, *crocodilarium*. It occurred to me to follow the example of those New York housewives; they didn't know what to do with the baby alligators that their children had brought from Florida as souvenirs of their December holidays. True, this isn't New York. But I thought that there must be a network of sewer-pipes beneath the city large enough to keep you happy. I read that you would live a hundred years if nothing extraordinary happened to you (what could be so extraordinary in one of the great African rivers?) and if your existence unfolded in a natural setting (how does one measure what's natural for a creature that begins its life in a pet shop in San Angel?). I also read that you'd never die of old age. If it weren't for accidents (someone killing you for your hide), you'd keep growing and would live forever. You're the closest thing to a god in the natural world. You'll be chatting with my great-grandchildren about us. Meanwhile, you walk along river-bottoms, where the water is unbreathable and you bump into a hippopotamus who's doing the same thing. You greet each other on the bottom where you walk. Good morning. Good morning. Upright like the two-legged animals that roamed the earth two hundred million years before the first man appeared. The image seemed so comic, and then so atrocious, that I tossed you into the toilet-bowl and pulled the chain. But everything changes in Africa's rivers, except you. You appeared in the shower downstairs, in the kitchen sink, in the water-tank. My husband and son were on your side. They placed you in the shower and seemed delighted by your company as they bathed. They assured me that soon we'd bring you to the zoo.

I'd like to see you blind, with opaque, half-closed eyes, almost non-existent, not like they are now, golden and, on the contrary, beautiful. You must have traveled up the current, or let yourself be dragged by it, to grab him by the legs or knock him down with your tail and then, although the water was shallow, drown him. It wasn't you who killed him, it was the water in your pool. Your rows of conical teeth serve poorly for such tasks. You let the water do what you couldn't. I should have killed you the way

4

they kill rats, in a cage, submerged in a bucket of water, leaving you there all night, or feeding you small poisoned animals. I imagined that you'd carried my son to the surface and in a grotesque dance, whirled like a top on your tail, holding his body by one of its limbs until you dismembered it. The pieces had to be small enough to fit down your gullet. You carried what remained to an underground cave; you submerged with the torso to the bottom where you imprisoned it under some heavy object. You returned to feed on the cadaver for days, sometimes weeks. . . . In my imagination, you repeated it again and again. One day, as you were weeping, I had a vision. My son was entering a kind of marsh. It was the place where you'd taken him. He would have been eleven or twelve, and he balanced himself in a canoe made from a carved tree-trunk in order to trap snakes with a long forked stick. I watch him perform a strange ritual: he presses the backs of the snakes' heads against a hard surface and then grabs them behind the jaw to milk them. There's a rope running the length of the stick that ends in a loop in case they manage to escape or he has to trap them in the water. He travels with a silent dog, passing through the swamp. He doesn't kill the snakes; he puts some in large canvas bags, extracts the poison from others, keeping their jaws open and stimulating the reflex that makes them surrender their liquid into a previously-labeled vial. Then he releases them in the water or on land in the same place he caught them. The image is starting to fade. I want to communicate with him but he doesn't hear or see me. It's as if he existed in another world. He's my son but he doesn't know it.

I don't think it's a good idea for you to approach me. I know that you want to put your snout in my lap, but I can talk to you from here. Next, you'll want to put on your goggles to swim underwater.

During one of your nights of weeping, I don't know how you convinced my son to enter the bathroom. We'd told him not to respond to your call because your behavior made us distrust you. We told Miguel you were like a rabid dog during the hours or numbered days of your desolation. We'd already put him to bed. Your weeping was unbearable and shrill. We decided to deliver you to the zoo the very next day. Your own noise enraged you, injured you, and your howls grew stronger, reaching their climax cyclically at certain hours of the day and night.

You place your head in my lap like a child or husband. My son. Do you want me to call you that? My love. Would you like me to scratch you here, behind your eyes? Do you want me to place a little gold ring in your ear? But don't cry anymore. And don't look at me like that. Pleading. You have the eyes of a fish. And you're growing heavy. Your head a thousand times heavier than your little body when we bought you. We paid a price that seemed extravagant for a pet. My voice consoles you, that's the only way you'll stop weeping. Was it because of that you asked me to keep you company? What have you done with my son? With my husband? I've entered because of you as well, I admit it, although at first your weeping seemed unbearable: we'd watch a movie with the volume turned up, listen to music, go for a drive although it was four in the morning, just not to hear you. These last few times I've awaited your outbursts with longing.

Caring for you, changing the water in your pool, obtaining animals for food . . . it was a routine, I felt like a zoo-keeper. We ignored each other. You dropped your pretension of acting like a pet a long time ago. All that mattered were your moments of delirium. For my husband, with his typical male reasoning, the most important thing was to solve the mystery of our son's disappearance and to find him. He entered to see if it would be possible to negotiate with you. I'm not reproaching you now. So many times I was about to kill you and trying to find the cruelest way to do it. You heard my reproaches and curses. I'm looking for my husband and my son, I feel their presence and nearness. Sometimes I feel that we've been lucky to know you. You've brought us to ruin. Do you think you could have brought us to any other end? I know that your pool is bottomless. I see the milky waters, at times your body looks colorless, and this isn't a bathtub's usual depth. I know that crocodiles don't have the strength to open their jaws. A child can hold them closed by the snout. Once open, their power is enormous. Once a crocodile captures its victim, only a miracle would allow it to escape. The moment I want to hold your snout closed, I'll know that my life is over. I ask this of you. Let it slip through my hands. Take me by the waist and submerge with me.

Metepec, January 12, 1991

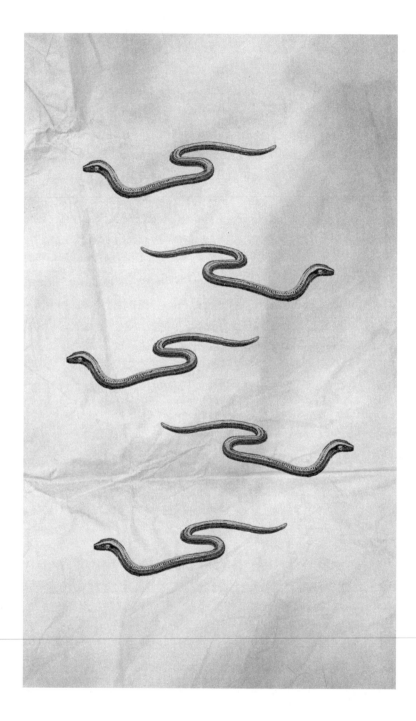

Snakes and Ladders

to René Solís Brun

The company's star salesman and now assistant manager of personnel got on well with the boss's son and although he didn't like the old man, he didn't have anything to worry about since Hernán González and Sons was now almost exclusively Sons and, given that the younger son had left after a fight with the older one over some marketing strategy, the important thing was for him to get along with the older González son. Marilú de la O Vilchis, the executive secretary, knew that the older González son respected Pedro Enciso, had offered him a Christmas bonus the previous year, included him from time to time in private board meetings, and almost always put his name on the list of outstanding employees of the month—whether as salesman or as assistant manager of personnel—and granted him the opportunity to take a countless number of training courses. Enciso was the best student in his Intermediate English class III B. He'd spent two years studying English, from seven to nine in the morning in the board-meeting room of Hernán González and Sons, together with other co-workers, who at the beginning of each level numbered eight and then began disappearing as the semester went on.

"If you do well in the English course, you could study Japanese," the older González son said to encourage him. He didn't have far to go: IV B, 5 b . . . and the same for levels six and seven.

Enciso had a future. That's what the older González son said and she, as the older González son's secretary, had no reason to disagree. Aside from that, she liked Enciso. He was a little overweight, was fond of long meals with many courses, was a chatterbox, had a thick mustache that after each fourth or fifth sip of coffee he brushed to either side with a tiny metal comb—an accessory on his *complete* Swiss army knife—he wore a gold chain, and had thin hair that stuck up as if anticipating the caresses of someone or of a Swiss army knife with a little larger comb or—why not?—a brush.

His wife was awful. Ugly. Devoid of sympathy. Badly dressed. Always reeking of cheap perfume or plain soap. She knew about those things. Half the salaries of the secretaries of Hernán González and Sons went directly from where the checks were printed to the safe at "Liverpool" department store. González and Sons had the appearance of a modeling school, an elegant café somewhere in the southern end of the city, a collection of respectable people (if somewhat overdressed), of well-to-do girls on their way to picking up their kids from school. They looked good, they smelled good and they talked trash—huddled in the ladies' room—about the wives and sometimes the daughters of the male employees. They also spoke terribly about each other and the competition was fierce.

The men, for their part, had a bet going as to who could sleep with the most female employees of González and Sons; getting them pregnant, according to how it was calculated, either counted as double or shut them out of the game. For the women, everything depended on *who* got them pregnant. One had to know how to choose, to have a strategy and not to lose heart because of the ups and downs in labor relations and the salary increases awarded for no apparent reason.

For her, Pedro Enciso was the one. She never rubbed it in his face but neither did she hide her interest. Moderate and coquettish, sensible and eloquent, if she happened to sit next to him in the dining room, she could spend half an hour making trivial, meaningless conversation, addressing everyone present, or she could be silent, or would blush at any off-color joke, and then, suddenly, with the arrival of another co-worker at the table and the need to rearrange the chairs to make room for him, she would let slip to Pedro the following phrase, accompanied by a gleeful laugh that could disarm anyone:

"Here I come, Pedrito."

Or

"I'm going to fall all over you."

One had to know how to wait for the right moment. For a population educated by *telenovelas*, waiting was not a problem. That's what Martín, the young, generally nasty, head of publicity told her.

Marilú feared that he might not go on the company picnic. He arrived, not alone but accompanied by others and she whispered in his ear as they arranged the knapsacks, balls, lunch-boxes and other belongings in the luggage compartment of the bus:

"Now you look like Pedro Enciso and Sons."

Her comment didn't seem to bother him.

It was afterwards, when it occurred to one of the men to head for the peak high above the place they'd chosen for lunch, that she saw her opportunity. Pedro Enciso's wife preferred to remain behind to prepare the meal, claiming that she couldn't go very far in high heels—who would think of going to a picnic in high heels?—so they left her sinking into the mud at the lake-shore, thought Marilú, as she withdrew with the rest without losing sight of Enciso. Everyone took a different route; according to the guy who thought up the idea—seconded by the special-events organizer for the company, who'd gone on ahead to set up the little numbered sheets of paper—there would be a prize for the first five who reached the top. Enciso entered by a trail from the other side of the creek, thinking he'd reach the peak from behind. She followed him without the others realizing it, and emerged from a clearing face-to-face with him, feigning surprise.

"Enciso, I believe you're lost."

"You're wrong. I plan on reaching the peak and watching the others as they come up."

"Can I go with you?"

"Yes, but I don't plan on sharing the prize."

"I doubt very much you'll get there first," said Marilú and broke into a run.

He pursued her, surprised, shouting for her to wait for him if she didn't want to get lost. At a given moment, she reclined against some mounds of grass on the hillside. Now's my chance, she thought. She raised her arms in a gesture that looked as though she were taking off her blouse, then she stretched and finally relaxed, supporting the nape of her neck with both hands. He looked at her breasts and the sweat stains at her armpits.

"Wouldn't you like to share something else?" asked Marilú.

"Yes," he said, after a moment of hesitation. He'd shifted his gaze. "But not here. Let's climb higher and get off the trail."

When he fell into the pit, she leaned over it and saw it was bottomless; light was visible only some distance below. She didn't dare scream. She was afraid that they would discover she'd been alone with him. She'd pretend not to have seen him since the moment of the departure, together at the lake, when everyone was heading toward the hill. She continued climbing toward the peak, frightened, amazed, but now thinking only about that goal which moments before had seemed a little absurd to her.

Actually, Isabel hadn't wanted to go; and at first, Pedro hadn't shown much interest either. The possibility of an excursion for their children and their obligation not to disappoint Sr. González finally decided them.

The bus was similar to the model she'd known so well during her years of primary and secondary school. Divisions, clans, and hierarchies were formed, all within a few square meters, there was singing and jokes were told, one of the women threatened to be sick if they didn't stop in Tres Marías for brunch, and then, rather than a flat-tire, the engine overheated and they all had to get out. It occurred to some wise guy—there's always one of them—to collect wildflowers and they had to wait for him to find the purple ones he'd seen at a bend in the road. Apart from a new radiator, the bus needed a change of shock absorbers, seats that weren't so hard, and more space between them so that a normal-sized adult could sit properly without his knees sticking out into the aisle or, if he found himself next to the window, having to open his legs like a compass. Nobody felt like returning in the same vehicle that same afternoon. Although to completely vanish, as her husband had done, was to foolishly take everything to an extreme. Seeing who could scale to the top of one of the peaks in record time would be a natural reaction of any adult traveling more than two hours with his knees stuck against his chin and his buttocks aching. To have done it not staying together, but each one choosing his own path, was a natural consequence of the desire to separate oneself from a forced camaraderie and a failed attempt to have a good time.

Now she was in her house, sipping tea with a childhood friend.

"Zempoala is a good place to disappear," her friend Alicia Guevara de Zorrilla told her. "I think your Pedrito fled with some lover. They must have made a plan to meet at Kilometer 3, let's say, on the Zempoala highway between Mexico City and Cuernavaca. From there, with fake documents and years' worth of secret savings, they left in the direction of some place where he could live incognito for five years while you were paid his life insurance policy."

"Don't be ridiculous, Ali," Isabel answered. "What was he going to live on? He didn't have as much saved as you think."

Alicia had never been convinced that Pedro Enciso Guzmán was a good husband for her friend. Two years and some months had now passed since his disappearance.

Marilú wasn't the type of person who could keep a secret. She didn't say she'd witnessed the accident, but did admit that she and Pedro Enciso Guzmán had agreed to get to know each other better during the contest. She said that they hadn't carried out their plan, although she said it in a way that encouraged one to assume the opposite. So that the matter seemed to be whether Pedro Enciso Guzman had left one widow or two. The executive secretary of González and Sons dressed somberly, choosing to wear only blacks, whites, and grays for such a long time that one felt almost tempted to approach her to offer condolence.

Rumors are made of a substance that's very unstable and hard to control. I thought of the word "volatile" to describe the phenomenon, but another image related to rising came to mind, and because of that, I discarded it. I happened to overhear, in different spots and from different people in the company, the idea that surely Enciso, upon falling into the pit, was burdened by his unfinished business with Marilú. There are grottos two thousand meters deep, said one of the employees. Others were of the opinion that he'd fallen off a cliff. When he understood that his boss's secretary was offering herself to him, he decided to accept. Without exchanging a word, he followed her, enjoying the way she moved, watching her and imagining what it would be like to take off her jeans. She joked, saying that he was falling behind and he, in order to show her it wasn't true and that in a few moments his stamina would amaze her, took two steps off the narrow trail and leapt forward, over one or two bushes, feeling thorns dragging his pant-leg, and at the instant he looked back searching for Marilú's face, he either disappeared into the pit, or fell off the cliff.

Or had sex, insisted another employee. He saw Marilú's face and took her hand, the two of them smiling, if not laughing (although they had to be discreet), Pedro thinking how close he was to having her underneath him, practically at the summit of one of the highest peaks of Tres Marías. Those who defended this third possibility (I included myself in the first group: the second option, just like the third one, didn't completely explain the disappearance of the body; aside from that, it seemed to me that there wouldn't have been enough time for the assignment at hand to be carried out before Marilú rejoined the others) made observations like the following: the altitude and the exertion would have accelerated their breathing, everything would flow faster and faster, their cries would seem like those of an eagle or falcon.

So, now we return to this: He disappeared into the pit, or fell off a cliff, or died from the effort of taking off Marilú's jeans, during intercourse, or as a result of the same action. People made these comments in the men's room or returning from the cafeteria.

Another variation began when one of our co-workers, a public accountant with the air of a know-it-all, said, as if talking about bad weather, that Pedro Enciso Guzmán had always wanted to put an end to his life.

"You mean, of course, his life with Isabel," said Alejandro, who considered himself a good friend of the missing man. He always used those words instead of "the deceased."

"No," said the public accountant, examining his fingernails, "I'm referring to his biological life."

"What do you mean?"

"There must have been some reason he was always exclaiming 'swallow me up, earth.'"

"But the expression 'swallow me up, earth' was something automatic, learned by heart, something he always used without wanting it to come true!"

"How can anyone be sure?" said the accountant. "He used to say it so vehemently."

Alejandro remained silent. Then he added: "More than dying, he wanted to change."

"What better way to change than to die?"

Now it occurs to me, sitting in Pedro Enciso's chair, that at another moment, seated on the other side of this desk, I told him the story about Genoveva. I didn't say much about my summer in San Diego, at age ten, in my aunt and uncle's house, but I did so in great detail. The rear garden, the terrace and the pool overlooked a ravine. My cousin and I took walks to the ravine on three occasions, always with the same motive. David, who was a year older than me, always had the same excuse ready in case his mother found out: he was looking for his baseball, the one autographed by one of his favorite players, which his father had hit over the fence early that summer. In reality what David wanted wasn't for me to help him look for the ball—if we found it along the way, great! Then his excuse wouldn't be a complete lie—but to show me something.

By the time I'd noticed the photos, we were almost on top of them, behind the house of one of the neighbors, scattered over a surface four or five meters from one end to the other, 20 or 30 centimeters deep in all, given the way the paper had settled. We squatted, or got on our knees above the images, a jigsaw puzzle of female sexes, thighs, backs, buttocks, faces. You could only make out an entire image if you raised it, freed momentarily from the others, although some had gotten stuck together because of the sun or from chemicals. Most of the photos were in black and white; the color in the others, with the exception of the most recent ones, had turned more coffee-hued or yellow, the paper gray or beige, as if by mimesis, making them blend in with the surrounding trees and dry grass. It was the details that impressed me: the vulvae and lips were layered, mollusk-like it seemed to me, their color deeper and darker than the surrounding skin; the different-colored hair and forms of the mons; the asses pear-shaped mostly, beneath the fabric and texture of skirts, some held partially by the wearer's hand to expose a part of herself, or totally bare; the smalls of the back; breasts, as diverse as the genitalia; napes of necks, turns of shoulders; faces mostly smiling or, rather, lips wide-opened, beautiful and surprisingly familiar against the hardness and whiteness of the teeth, close to, next to, touching the softness and humidity of mouths. I felt dizzy and as if I were going to slide down the ravine any moment given the paper's slickness. We said nothing. The blood pumped between my eyes and I felt short of breath. I also remember that my mouth was dry, my lips and tongue felt odd. Maybe an outsider, a third party, would have described me as quiet or still. David looked at me and pointed his finger in a gesture that was an attempt at playfulness, knowledgeable camaraderie, but somehow seemed shy and didn't conceal his amazement despite the uncountable times he'd visited the site. It was clear to both of us that I had been somehow initiated into a mystery that had previously only been his. After that, we never spoke about what we'd seen, and returned on two more occasions, without saying where we were going although it was clear to both of us.

My aunt had forbidden us to go to the ravine because of her almost religious fear of snakes. According to her, what the photographer put in front of his house was trash to be picked up by the garbage truck, exactly the same as that of the other neighbors on the block.

We didn't see a single snake in the ravine, although we did see them in the garden, when they crossed it toward the pool to drink water, or sometimes to immerse themselves. They proved to be excellent swimmers, each slithering over the water as if propelled—a boomerang but in zig-zag, advancing between two rail-like lines—keeping its head slightly raised, like a lady who doesn't want to get her hair wet, but without the awkwardness, and without the need to stroke with arms. I believe that they did it because of the dryness, not their bodies' but the summer's, to free themselves momentarily from their efforts, the ravines, the earth, the parched grass, the eucalyptus leaves.

When Genoveva entered the room, David was reading in his bed, and I was seated at the desk solving some math problems with my cousin Jose, the youngest and my favorite. I was helping her because if she managed to figure out the total spent on groceries at the supermarket, my aunt would buy her a gift. She was seven but very precocious. I'd never seen Genoveva in her brother's bedroom. She was thirteen, which set her apart from us quite a bit.

Now she took a few steps into the room and stopped. She looked at us without moving and without saying anything. She wore a light white-cotton nightgown and unbuttoned it just enough to let it fall around her feet, without bending or breaking her stare.

Her breasts looked like a girl's, like two small cups, but her nipples, large and dark, were already a woman's. She didn't have much pubic hair but it seemed like more because it was dark and thick. She looked me in the face and I had the impression that she'd smiled at me. From the side, with her head slightly tilted, as if from behind her hair. The gesture also seemed sorrowful to me. There was something mad about it. I felt desire but I didn't know what to do. Finally, she stepped outside the circle of her nightgown, squatted to pick it up, and left the room.

"She's crazy," Jose said.

It made her laugh and I believe that David and I laughed, too.

"What did she want you to do?" Enciso asked me.

"I don't know," I responded. "Look at her, I guess."

I ask myself: do I really know how long I'll stay in this position? This last bit, more than a rumor, is an observation that personally seemed very wise to me. Don Leandro, who's been around longer than any of us, effectively carrying out his duties as head of the warehouse—which places him in the very bowels of the company—summarizes everything that's happened in the following way: "If you're going to work in a family business, it's best to belong to the family."

Toad's Visits

to Alicia García Bergua

The moment that Toad stopped visiting our family is clearer to me than the moment of his first appearance. I never understood the exact relationship between him and my mother. The princess (my mother) and a toad who should turn into a prince when he's kissed by the princess but who doesn't stop being a toad. The princess's frustration grows and she ends up cursing all amphibians. At a certain point that story was tossed into the wicker trunk in the corner of the bedroom, to be given away, along with some garments and hand-me-down toys still in one piece, as a gift to poor children when the cover no longer closed. But it's what happened before this that I'll try to explain now.

Her relationship with Toad wasn't simple; she shared the amphibian's metamorphosis and it seemed as if my mother was also a creature who, having lived only in water, was now seeking air. I sensed that she was a creature of two worlds. I knew little about her aquatic world; sometimes I saw her fleeting, orange-tinged image just below the surface. My father would experience something similar; even worse, he was a man who needed reasons in order to live—that is, he needed an explanation that arose from an action, one that was thorough and plausible regarding any irrational behavior or hair-brained idea. That night the four of us were sitting on the bed—the fourth one was my sister, so young then that I doubt she remembers much of what I'm about to tell; maybe she does but very differently, using the clairvoyance granted by childhood—and when he heard my mother's comments, my father began asking his questions and it was as if my sister and I stopped existing or found ourselves in another room. I didn't really understand what they were talking about but I was able to catch the last part.

"It's that when I'm not writing I feel very bad," my mother confessed and suddenly became very sad and I thought she was going to cry. "I feel like a frog. Even worse, like a toad in a fish-tank that must be fed."

My father laughed softly, hugging her.

"I feel numb," my mother continued. "Or like a pill dissolving in water. I'm like the witch in *The Wizard of Oz*! I melt and dis-appear, and I hate that feeling."

I thought that I didn't remember any book called *The Wizard of Oz*, let alone one with a witch in it, and would have to ask my mother to read it to us.

Thus began Toad's life in our family. I understood that it wasn't about whether being a toad is worse than being a frog. My first definition of a toad was more or less the following:

a. It wasn't a person.

b. Even less, a pet.

c. It was somehow related to my mother. My mother felt like a toad when she wasn't writing. The pic-ture was becoming clearer and I didn't like it one bit. It also didn't help that my parents wouldn't speak about him in front of us, although there was no lack of coded language or references, oblique, veiled glances accompanied by explanatory gestures which seemed somehow related to that strange presence. My mother wrote so she wouldn't feel like a toad. I even concluded that she wrote so she wouldn't turn into a toad, a possibility much more terrifying than the previous one.

At first, all this had nothing to do with our routine: we were very happy. At times we had to keep quiet or play in the garden, or go to the home of one of our friends after school, where my father picked us up after nightfall, or we'd spend the weekend with our grandparents; still, my mother's strange work didn't make her less affectionate or less attentive toward us. It was nice to know that we were different from the rest of our friends and that gave us a certain pride, like the boy who'd accompanied his parents on an African safari (to hunt animals? my mother asked, indignant), or the boy who came to school on a motorcycle, with his father, each of them wearing a helmet (he's a teenager, my father remarked, meaning the man), without ever breaking our routine of children in pre-school, and later, in the first years of primary school.

Toad stopped interesting us. But then an important change took place. And will Toad be coming today? asked my father. His question seemed strange, now that we hadn't spoken his name in a long time. He'd asked it in a moment of distraction or because of something urgent I didn't understand. They'd been arguing a lot in the last few days. I knew that my mother hadn't been able to write because she kept us company, in a bad mood, in the house or other places, instead of shutting herself in her studio, where the only sound we heard was the sound of her electric typewriter, sometimes mixed with the classical music she listened to. An important change took place in my appreciation of Toad. He really existed. As something alien from my father and mother. I pictured him next to her desk. He was big and imposing. When my mother shut herself in her room, I felt tempted to burst into that space—it was a fun place, full of all kinds of things (photos, seashells, stones, books, the typewriter, the record player, paintings, records, mementos, gifts from her grandparents, now dead . . .), most of the time in such disarray that it impressed my friends, since my mother liked to work on the floor, surrounded by papers and writing tools and correcting, or she pinned manuscript pages to the walls in order to cross out words or shorten passages, move them from one place to another. It always seemed that she was happiest in an atmosphere where disorder ruled. When I couldn't stand it any longer, I knocked on the door, or sometimes I entered without warning. If she wanted me to leave, all she had to do was not look at me and continue as if I weren't there, or she'd say: "Juan, not now, my love." If she looked at me, it was an invitation to come closer and, as I sat in her lap or in a chair by her side, we'd talk or listen to music, or I'd ask her questions. When she was the one who opened the door and went out, it meant that she'd finished her work for the time being and I'd look for her, or she, me, to play. Later, my sister, now a little older, would join our games, which at first seemed too rough to her. Wrestling, hide-and-seek, imitating different animals . . . we crawled all over the studio and the bedrooms or tussled on the carpet and bed. As she confessed to us many times, she liked to feel us, hug us, tickle us and hear us laugh.

But now I would enter fearfully, spying on her, sure that she wasn't alone. One day, I was playing hide-and-seek with my friend when I heard my mother crying—I'd hidden behind a huge flowerpot, on the terrace near the studio. She was crying very emotionally but, at the same time—which disturbed me more—in a silent, hushed voice. Manuel shouted my name but I didn't want to move. I was sure that Toad was visiting her and I wanted to look into the studio but the curtains were drawn. Night was already falling and when I came out of my hiding place, I lied to Manuel and my sister—who by then had stopped looking for me and were playing something else—telling them I'd fallen asleep.

A terrible period followed. The door to the studio, white with darker wood-grains and decorated with little iron stars, suddenly became threatening. My mother was very nervous, she often argued with my father, and she was often angry with the servants. We saw her only fleetingly, to the point that sometimes she asked them to bring up her meals to her bedroom, and she didn't have dinner with my father in the family room. It didn't last long but it seemed like forever.

One night, when I got up to go to the bathroom, my parents were talking in their bedroom. I didn't turn on the light so they wouldn't realize I was there and I sat on the toilet listening to what they were saying. My mother spoke softly but very emotionally, her words emphatic, sad, convulsive, and then she'd fall silent. There was also weariness in her voice. My father seemed to be consoling her. I knew—I don't know how, but I was absolutely sure—that they were talking about Toad. I could make out an occasional phrase. Something about the lack of peace and the suddenness of his visits. He dominated her, making her feel as if she might lose control and do something violent. Two words at the end of a sentence became engraved in my memory: "something terrible." I began to hate him. What was he demanding of my mother? Why did he visit her? Why did he make her cry? I didn't understand why my father didn't do something. Couldn't he prevent Toad from seeing her? I felt the same thing I'd picked up in my mother's voice: a mixture of guilt and fear.

One night I woke up. My mother was screaming. I went to their bedroom. My father was hugging her although she was beside herself, moving her arms and legs, and she didn't stop screaming. I was crying and my sister, frightened and silent at first, began crying, too. My father was shouting for Mercedes to come, and when she appeared, he ordered her to take us to her bedroom until he said otherwise. I yelled and kicked, I believe I bit Meche, I wanted to get free and attack Toad, kill him, escape with my mother, fling him into the street, hug her and calm her down, tell her that I loved her. I imagined all kinds of things, Toad behind the door, thousands of eggshells, my mother turned into a toad, drowning, buried by all those eggs, but Meche was stronger than I was and managed to pull me away. My sister, maybe out of fear, was very docile.

I don't know what happened after that. I heard sirens and we saw different-colored lights on the window although Meche had drawn the curtains so we wouldn't see either the house or the garden. Meche said that Sebastián, who worked in the house as a gardener, a messenger and sometimes a driver, must be helping my father and that my mother was better now because she wasn't screaming. We heard strangers' voices, a lot of noise, the sound of engines and then nothing.

Meche stayed in our bedroom that night and very early in the morning, before dawn, my father entered the room, hugged us, and we all cried together. He said that my mother would return to us soon.

"And Toad?" I asked him.

I saw that my father wanted to ask me, "what toad?" but he only looked at me, then at Mercedes.

"I haven't heard anything about toads, sir," she said.

"I know." He remained silent and then reached out his arms to draw me toward him. "No one wishes your mother harm, either her or either of you." He kissed my sister.

That was Toad's death sentence, although it took a long time for him to die. It was very different having my mother at a great distance, outside the house, than just a few yards away, with only a half-open door in-between. The wait was long and it was only when I saw her arrive and hugged her that I stopped feeling afraid.

We never mentioned Toad again. My mother was better. Occasionally she went away for periods of one or two weeks, vacations she took alone although later my father would join her, and she returned rested but a little saddened. Sometimes her eyes were full of grief. It was the trace of her other life, the aquatic one, and the amphibians that reminded her of it.

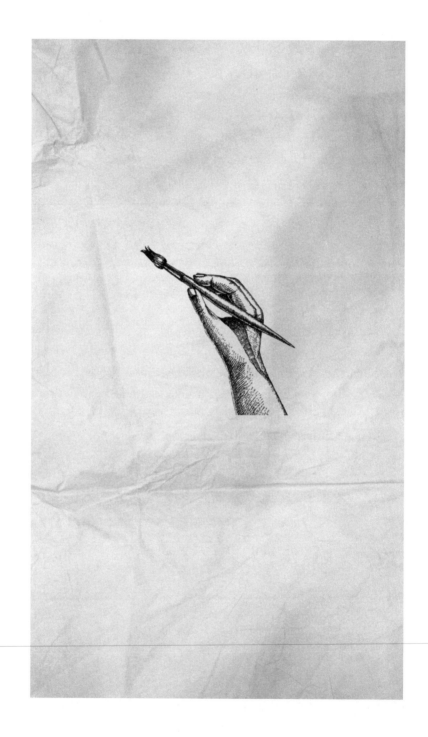

Three Figures and a Dog

to Jaime Lagúnez Otero, dear friend and brother

He liked to be in the chapel at dawn and also in the afternoon when something similar, though not identical, occurred. For that to happen, he had to leave home when his wife got up to milk the cow. He'd finally wake up as he put his hand into the bucket next to the well and wiped his face. He usually carried a loaf of bread, a piece of onion, and sometimes a little cheese, wrapped in a handkerchief. He'd leave his brushes, pencils, paints and other tools in a corner of the chapel, behind some stones that hadn't been used during its construction. He didn't paint at that hour. He was waiting for the right color. He'd observe the sky and mix paints in a small clay vessel, smudging them with his finger, measuring quantities, adding water or oil or, on one occasion, wine. He imagined that if the wine was his blood and the blue of the sky he was seeking was the Virgin's color, and the Virgin was his mother and if he and the Virgin were of the same blood, then maybe . . .

Sometimes the abbot made his rounds to study the painting's progress. At the beginning he was very patient. After weeks in which the master painter didn't do anything and the wall looked the same, the abbot asked the artist about his method, since he noticed no craft in what he saw. He'd hired him because he knew his work from the time when he still belonged to a workshop in the city. However, because he couldn't count on resources, payment was promised when he finished the painting and, for the very same reason, he hadn't specified a date.

"The craft is over there," said the master painter, pointing toward the cypresses and the sky.

"If you're waiting for it to fall from heaven. . . ," said the abbot and left his sentence unfinished, cutting it off by slowly shaking his head.

"It's not the craft that I'm waiting for, but a certain color. Once I have the color, the figures will simply appear."

"The background means more than the figures to you? Who's ever heard such nonsense! And what are you thinking of painting? Angels, saints . . . or a color? I've asked you for saints, not a color."

The master didn't say anything now, so he wouldn't further anger the abbot. There would be saints but those would come later, with that blue as a background—to give them courage, since painted any other way they'd turn their backs and return to where they came from. He observed the old man for a moment; all in all, even with his wrathful nature, he was a good and wise man.

Facing the respectful silence of the master painter, the abbot said, before leaving: Close your eyes. The images will come to you from here.

And he touched the place where his heart would be with the index and middle fingers of his right hand.

After the sun cleared the horizon, the master painter had nothing to do. Since he still hadn't discovered the color, he had breakfast and walked from one end of the chapel to the other, singing softly to warm himself up a little. He lost time in unnecessary ruminations.

With the color he'd know what he needed to paint, what form to give the saints, everything, but even so he observed the wall and imagined what he'd fill it with.

He used to return home, to his chores in the country and at the workshop, eat with his wife, and go back to the chapel in the afternoon. He preferred twilight at that hour. The blue of May in the great, joyous moments before nightfall had more than once moved him to tears. It seemed like a sign from Heaven, María's cloak, fragrant, pulsating and warm, a passage to another reality whose fleetingness he was grateful for because had it lasted any longer it might have led him to something that could turn from ecstasy into terror, something related to death or insanity.

The abbot returned to visit him in the mornings, now that his anger had subsided; at most he'd threaten to look for another painter, even one from another town, to do the fresco. The master painter always responded the same way to him: before the end of summer, he'd have the painting completed. To his wife he'd say that the fresco was progressing and that the abbot was very happy with his work.

Months passed. The wind began blowing differently. The wheat harvest was approaching. The only thing the master painter had done was add more lime to the wall. In his life there was only his wife—two of his daughters had died a long time ago, and two others lived in the city with an uncle, learning everything related to manufacturing and selling cloth—the abbot, and a dog that waited for him on the other side of the bridge to accompany him to the chapel in the morning and return with him at night to the same place. Sometimes he crossed paths with a stranger; or he or Teresa offered lodging to pilgrims; except for that they lived alone. That's how he wanted it; they could have moved to the city where they'd lived for many years. But he longed for that solitude, he felt it necessary at that moment, and his life revolved around the wall, he returned to the wall time and again, although he hadn't stopped doing other tasks requested of him in his visits to the workshops. He never managed to interest the dog in accompanying him home and where it came from was a mystery, since the painter and his wife had no neighbors for many kilometers around them; besides, it was strange that an animal so small could survive on its own in a region rife with wolves. Furry, with short legs and a big, round head, it wagged what remained of its tail—the other part seemed to have been left in a trap—every time it saw the master painter, although it never barked. The master was the one who spoke, in a loud, untiring voice. On one occasion, it occurred to him that his life was like what he hoped to achieve in his painting: some figures and an enormous blue sky. The blue had to hold the last light of the sun, a yellow as liquid and brilliant as gold. I will paint three figures, he thought one morning, pacing from one side of the chapel to the other, followed by the eyes of the dog, who preferred to accompany him that way instead of having to walk. He thought about Teresa, the abbot, and himself.

"I'll include you, too!" he said, looking at the dog and laughing.

The dog wagged its tail.

That day he painted the dog and didn't return home until it was time to eat. The dog accompanied him on his return to the bridge and remained there. In the afternoon, tired, the master painter considered not returning to the chapel. It would be the first afternoon he didn't do so. He lay down but after a while, didn't feel well and ran to the bridge, promising himself he'd reach the chapel even if it were only to see the twilight. The dog wasn't on the bridge waiting for him; this saddened him and it seemed to suggest something, whether good or bad, he didn't know. He stopped there, looking toward the sun, but night fell swiftly and it was preferable, he thought, not to arrive at the chapel just to get there with the last daylight falling at his back. In the blue instant that transported him, he lowered his gaze to the river, to a spot not so deep where the sandy bottom could be seen. The color of the sky was also there. He realized that he needed dark brown, a bit of black, gold like the sand at the river-bottom in order to be able—together with the mixture he already had—to reproduce the color!

He ran toward home. Everything was happening in a rush. It seemed to him that the stars were moving and that the moon had risen in the sky more quickly than on other nights. He arrived shouting and half-explained to his wife the cause of his frenzy. She wanted to go with him, but he preferred that she didn't since he really didn't know what might happen. He collected the necessary things to light the wall, various pigments and oils that he flung in a haversack together with the bread, ham and grapes and, with the blanket over his shoulder that Teresa had insisted on, he left.

He achieved the color, although only with the light of day would he know for sure. He gazed at his palm by the light of the lantern. The wall wasn't large but preparing it and the paint, combined with applying a thick, even coat, took him many hours. He missed the dog and worked around its figure, taking care to make it appear as if it were painted after the blue. When he finished, he ate some food with a hearty appetite, feeling great satisfaction. He thought about retuning home, but his desire to see the blue wall when dawn came made him decide to spend the night there. He wrapped himself in the blanket and leaned against the opposite wall, facing the door that he left open so

33

the sun would wake him, without caring if the wolves or some bear entered. He fell asleep planning the figure that he'd begin to paint the next day.

When he woke in the morning, the wall looked like smooth, liquid gold, like water in the well at certain times. The light struck the wall obliquely, so the master painter—whose legs had fallen asleep—dragged himself a few yards over so he could see it from another angle. A change occurred as the master painter moved along the floor. The gold became blue, the same color as the sky that he now saw through the window. There then appeared—it was impossible to know if what he saw had already been there or only became visible because of the glow and the new angle— three figures. They seemed a little frightened, as if they were pre- senting themselves for the first time.

The master observed them and then began shouting, weeping, speaking like someone possessed, without knowing what he was saying or in what language. They were angels! No. They were saints! No. They looked like men but they also could be women. Two of them seemed more masculine and the other feminine, although the three figures were dressed similarly, with long tunics that covered part of their faces and almost reached their bare feet. The figure on the left had his left arm raised and the other hand held, at the height of his thigh, the fallen hand of the central figure—the woman?—who with her free hand grasped her tunic at heart-level. The other figure, on the right, clasped his hands on his abdomen and tilted his head gently upward. The three figures looked forward, their legs not together but separated, as if they were walking. The master felt them com- ing toward him, toward the chapel's interior, toward the world. Where did they come from? He didn't know. He'd tell the abbot that they were God's emissaries. It gave him great pleasure that the color was there, behind them and in front of him, so that he could always look at it, no matter what time of day. He knelt and offered an Our Father and three Hail Mary's in thanks and went running to tell Teresa. He wanted her to be the first one to see his blue and the handiwork of God.

All of it: years of study; months of work; the original discovery, spontaneous and gratifying; the fifth summer workshop for foreigners or nationals interested in art history or in restoration—most attended with the goal of fulfilling a requirement to obtain the master's degree, above all from U. S. universities, and so they arrived in Florence for the three summer months when Doctor Giovanni Lombardi was available to accompany them to the Tuscan countryside (it was more like *they* accompanied *him*) and allow them to observe how he applied his knowledge of fresco restoration on the eastern wall of a small chapel (when they actually did something, it was *exactly* what he asked them to do)—; his reputation as a specialist of Thirteenth- and early Fourteenth-century Italian art . . . in short, the result of his wager, of the passion with which he'd sensed that the stains under the dampness and earth in that chapel were figures, and not just any ones, but the work of a great master, whose skill was displayed, in part, by the traces of various colors he'd managed to discover (above all a blue and another color, a strange one, a gold like he'd never seen before); from the fourth figure, small and to one side, Lombardi had extracted browns and blacks and, because it seemed to lend itself more to his research, he'd worked more on that one, finally concluding it was a dog; for that reason, when he requested a subvention from the Italian government and from various U. S. universities—it wasn't for nothing that he put up with, year after year, the post-graduate students, in general, individuals he'd forget a month after dealing with them and besides that, they irritated him with their terrible Italian, their shallow ideas about art, and their adolescent manners—he'd titled his discovery "Three Figures and a Dog"... all of it would be seen as it truly was the next morning. The canvas looked like an enormous piece of gauze; smeared beforehand with a solution he'd perfected himself that should absorb—or have absorbed in the 72 hours it had been hanging, stuck to the fresco as if it were a skin, and compressed with an enormous board—instead of blood, dirt, dust, pollen, flyspecks, incense, saliva, sweat and other kinds of moisture, hair and the dry skin of generations of pilgrims . . . everything that wasn't part of the fresco, of the layer of lime, sand and marble dust, the pigments, and who knows what other ingredients used by the painter at the moment of his creation.

He'd seen enough to be deeply moved. Without being religious, what he'd felt was something that only could be described in religious terms. They were, without a doubt, human figures; or maybe angels without wings; maybe saints without haloes, dressed in the manner of Jews at the time of Christ. This increased Lombardi's interest: medieval painters had no way of knowing what clothing in Biblical Palestine looked like. Speaking of influences—although he preferred not to because he felt as if he were facing something unique—Byzantium and Sicily immediately came to mind, the works of certain monasteries he'd seen in Greece, Bulgaria, and Russia when he was writing his doctoral thesis, much more than Italian art. As with every great work of art, it belonged to its moment, but it also seemed to have fallen out of the sky. It seemed a precursor, dark and almost accidental, of Cimabue and Giotto. The most amazing thing was that everything suggested that the fresco, under the layers that had accumulated with the passing centuries, was perfectly preserved. That, together with the discovery of the colors, had him in a worse state than a father who awaits the birth of his child and, though he tried to hide it, he couldn't sleep and went several days almost without taking a single bite. He waited anxiously for the dawn.

He was the first one to enter and it seemed odd to see a dog sitting in the corner. It wagged what was left of its tail and looked at him. Lombardi had never liked animals but felt obliged to approach it and give it a few pats on the head. Everything was in its place so it would have been impossible for the dog to have entered—the windows, high in addition to being small and few, two on each side, were all sealed; and the other door, unopened since he'd discovered the place, was closed with its usual padlock. His assistants swore that they hadn't entered the chapel at night after he'd locked it up, or seen the animal before.

"Or it entered before I left and I didn't notice it," thought Giovanni, "or Chris and Laura came here last night and didn't completely close the door."

The tent, big and with individual cots inside, didn't permit the intimacy some students wanted—normally two, one of each sex . . . although during the years he'd spent bringing them to this place, that hadn't been the only combination. He'd prohibited his assistants, in no uncertain terms, from entering the chapel at night, given the advanced stage of the work in progress, but it wasn't the first time that they preferred to have sex there instead of on the grassy hills under a full moon, at an hour when the weather was most agreeable.

The dog, in the end, was the least of it. They prepared everything to remove the canvas, which looked like an enormous painting stretched over an equally wide frame in such a way that the separation would be uniform when it was pulled with the same effort from all points; for that purpose Giovanni had designed a mechanism with wheels and a kind of block, with pulley-wheels fixed to the frame every 50 centimeters, and the central pulley placed at the height of one of the windows, right in the middle of the opposite wall.

The canvas seemed stuck to the fresco, which alarmed Giovanni, but the adhesion lasted only a fraction of a second. When he separated it, Giovanni thought that it was like making a giant photocopy. More to the point, that was his fear. According to his calculations, the liquid should only help absorb the surface material. Still, how could he know—except by chemical analysis, from (incomplete) knowledge of the materials that were used in that era—what was and wasn't on the surface? His solution was, at most, a flip of a coin even though he might swear that the coin had only one side.

He suddenly experienced a phenomenon similar to what he'd felt as a child, when during a sailing excursion with his family they'd caught a dorado and the moment they pulled it out of the Caribbean waters, when not only he but also his parents and sister were shouting, for an instant he'd seen the beauty of the greens, yellows, reds, blues . . . metallic and slippery, the play between the elements of fire and water (he now recognized the similarity between the blue and the gold of the fresco and his childhood memory), before the captain struck the head of the fish with a mallet, causing the colors to immediately take flight, followed all too soon by a grayish hue, like death, settling into its skin.

He thought that on this occasion life hadn't disappeared with spilled blood but with the vanished colors. For a moment he believed he could see the fresco as it must have been the first time the painter stood back to contemplate it. After his jaw dropped and his hands rose and fell from the emotion of his discovery, he began to scream: the figures disappeared at the very moment of separation, as if they'd existed between a scab and now-healthy skin. Later his assistants would say no, they'd seen nothing, nothing except the blue, absolutely stupendous. Imbeciles! Most of them had careers as civil engineers and in order to choose the easiest subjects, meet other young people and travel, they'd registered for Renaissance Studies, for example.

It wasn't that the blue wasn't stupendous; it was much more than that. By itself it was worth much more than murals five times its size and infinitely more occupied. Yes, "occupied" was the right word. The way someone asks: "May I occupy this seat?" However, he'd seen the other. Besides, what would they say about him? He feared that they might see this as a failure. "Your *thinner* worked very well," they'd say ironically. "Your solution has resolved everything." "*Dissolved*," a third one would say. The art magazines would comment on the loss in their editorials, reasoning thus: "With a color like this, what might the painter not have painted?" The tabloids, more sensationalized, would run the headline: "We've gained a color and lost a masterpiece." The tourist guides would show the fresco as what could have been.

He stared at the reverse side of the enormous canvas, seriously doubting he'd find something—what he'd seen wasn't something that could be separated, lifted off with a Kleenex, that could be cleaned with an enormous sanitary pad ("what a strange idea!" he thought)—and, effectively, as he'd later prove in the laboratory, he discovered everything he'd hoped to find—earth, fungi, smoke residues, human skin and eyelashes and other kinds of hair, insect wings, fly specks and also bat guano—but nothing extraordinary. Now an immense fatalism settled into him. "We've been left without art," he thought out loud.

His assistants tried to lift his spirits.

"*Blue on blue*," said Chris, trying to sound clever.

"Three figures and a dog," murmured Laura.

"Well, for now, there's the dog," said Mónica, the Spaniard, smiling as if to suggest that the matter wasn't so serious and pointing at the dog that, in fact, continued sitting there.

Viola di Bordone

to Ignacio Padilla

When Margarita, who'd been his wife's best friend, told him that playing CDs was like having musicians performing their pieces right in front of you in your living room, Javier looked skeptical. Margarita's passion as she described the CD's fidelity to Mozart's *Requiem* seemed to him, for lack of a better word, adolescent. The host unfolded his hands in his lap to rest them on the chair's arms. He uncrossed his legs only to cross them again, this time the right one over the left. Yet this little exercise, poor and clumsy, as Javier himself was the first to recognize, succeeded in leading them out of the *impasse* Margarita had tried to steer them toward. Margarita changed the subject with a quick glance at her watch and a request to use the phone to call her daughter. Javier took advantage of that to stand up. He thought that, in reality, they were far from being close. But that wasn't the reason for his sudden sadness; the sensation arose, rather, from an alternate scenario in which Lilian, his wife, was still alive.

The telephone call allowed Margarita to leave with the same haste she'd arrived in. She's a life-saver, thought Javier. Before leaving, Margarita placed a little gift in his hands, somehow reinforcing the impression. Instead of medication, or a book that he *must* read, or a sandwich wrapped in aluminum foil from some delicatessen (Javier never knew if it was left over from some meal or a special order), this time it was a compact disk.

"Thank you, Margarita," he told her, saying good-bye with two kisses. He added, alluding to the fact that he didn't have the equipment to listen to it, "I'll have to shelve it in the bookcase."

"That's your problem," said Margarita, wanting to sound ironic although there was some resentment in her voice.

Javier almost didn't wait for the elevator doors to close before turning around and returning to his apartment. He had the unpleasant and persistent sensation of having received help from the Salvation Army. As Margarita left the building and asked the doorman to get her car, Javier served himself a double whiskey on the rocks and thought that Margarita had felt compassion for the widower who folded and unfolded, crossed and uncrossed his hands and legs; like those hotel managers who leave a copy of the New Testament on the bureau beside the bed, she'd presented him with Haydn's *Trios for Baritone*. He liked the shape of that little disk, its cover, its shininess like mirrored platinum. He rested it on his index finger and then returned it to its case in order to shelve it with the *long-play* records he barely listened to so it wouldn't be in the way. As compensation, he put on something by Haydn, the *Concert for Oboes in D major*, on the old record-player. He returned to the sofa.

A strange affection for that disk of Haydn's *Trios for Baritone* took hold of him, like someone who grows fond of a paperweight, geode, or candlestick. Besides, because of its shape and its location, both a little bit absurd, instead of forgetting the object when passing by the shelf, he took it down, opened the case and toyed with the disk. It never occurred to him to buy the equipment to play it. He finally listened to the recording when a

44

friend lent him his car, fully equipped and with a compact-disk player—state-of-the-art that year and enormous—to take a trip. When he saw that the musical selection wasn't too much to his liking and, at best, bored him quickly, he decided to take along the gift from his wife's friend.

He didn't listen to any other disk, during either his departing or return trip. She'd been right; the sound was good, even better. But what seemed laughable to him was the idea expressed by Margarita that the new technology was able to capture and retransmit music, as if listening to a compact disk were the same as attending a live concert; neither could he accept the idea that the great interpreters who were either elsewhere at the moment or deceased could, in this way, continue being present. He'd have to tell Margarita that the only certainty of her entire theory was the fact that in the recording of Haydn's *Trios for Baritone*, one could make out, with spine-tingling clarity, the breathing of one of the musicians. He must have been catching a cold. That thought made Javier laugh out loud. He also felt alone: he was the only one traveling along the highway at night.

What had seemed comical to him at first became, as he listened to the complete compact disk, a disturbing experience now that the breathing which revealed itself at moments was also a silent, continual presence that added feeling and beauty to the music. One could say that the most perfect aspect of the entire work was the phrasing of the breathing. He took the CD cover, a kind of explanatory booklet in English and German, and leafed through it in spite of the fact that he'd almost completely memorized the text and the photo of the musicians; he used the weak light inside the car to study the three men, who appeared in black-and-white because of the photo and their tuxedos, without being able to identify the one responsible for the breathing.

45

It turned out that the voice wasn't coming from one of the three musicians, but from the instrument, a viola di bordone, played by the musician Balázs Kakuk. That decided him, with a burst of emotion, after he'd listened to the disk many times at the homes of different friends in order to isolate the instruments as much as possible. He began getting more interested in the catalogues of different CD companies, specialty magazines, programs of the major trios, quartets, chamber orchestras . . . The viola di bordone, built in 1756, although originally from Vienna, could now be found in a museum in Budapest. Balázs Kakuk was one of three musicians who'd been granted the privilege of using the instrument, above all for tours through Western Europe, especially Germany and, on rare occasions, through some cities in the United States. Javier looked at the program and decided that the closest one, in distance and time, would be a presentation of the chamber orchestra of Hungary in one of the courtyards at the Art Institute of Chicago. He called a travel agency and made the necessary reservations.

He managed to sit very close to the musicians. After the program, he went out into the cold Chicago night convinced that the viola di bordone had been breathing. His certainty had something feverish and delirious about it. He collected, in the course of the following six months, almost all the available recordings made with that instrument and it was the only thing he listened to. The breathing repeated itself from one interpretation to another.

One day he wanted to know if the instrument only breathed when they were playing, a matter that could only be known by the three men now closest to it and by the countless musicians who had once played it. He was able to follow the trio, the same one from the original CD, to three European cities, and attended each one of the programs, to the point that it seemed as if the musicians recognized him. Balázs Kakuk had worn an expression that suggested jealousy to Javier: on one occasion, when he wanted to approach to touch the instrument and see it more closely, the musician had two guards called to remove him.

More than two years have now passed since Margarita's fateful visit. Javier is seated in a chair at the People's Hotel in Budapest and spins the compact disk around his right index finger. It's an object as familiar to him as his wedding ring. He thinks again about the difficulty of sharing a passion for something. It's not that one person can be the only one who's sensitive but that everyone is sensitive in a different way. This seems even truer with music. Even with Lilian, whom he'd felt so close to, it was rare when they had the same reaction after listening to a certain phrase or fragment or a complete movement. Sometimes the only possible communion was to appreciate and recognize the other person's passion. It's also true that such a passion isn't entirely comprehensible to oneself, much less so being a matter of will.

The first night of his stay at the hotel he had a little argument with the manager on the night shift—it later turned out that he was also the manager of the day shift—Mr. Kárkányi, when he came down to the reception desk to complain that there was no hot water to take a bath. When he'd wanted to use the telephone he'd also discovered that the cable disappeared under the bed without reaching the wall. Mr. Kárkányi, phlegmatic and courteous, listened to all the complaints of the gentleman guest as he thumbed through, and for a few moments studied, the card file.

"Impossible," he said, half-pulling one of the cards out of the box.

47

After twenty minutes of arguing, the manager excused himself and disappeared in the room behind the reception desk. He returned accompanied by a woman whom he'd obviously awakened. He spoke with her in Hungarian, in front of Javier, and after repeating the same question several times and making her repeat her answers (all of it unintelligible to Javier), he turned to him and one more time, in French, although addressing him now as "Distinguished Guest" and not "Mr. Guest," he said:

"This *mademoiselle* is the chambermaid in charge of the floor where you have your room. She herself made the beds and cleaned there this morning and she assures me that your room has been inspected and that everything is in order. Are there towels in the bathroom?"

"Yes, of course."

"Then, there's also hot water."

Javier might have continued arguing until dawn if necessary but the woman looked exhausted. He thought that if he changed rooms, someone would have to make the bed, hang up the towels . . .

Javier went to bed without taking a bath.

He'd only been asleep for a little while when he heard someone knocking on the door. He looked at his watch: it was six-thirty in the morning. Feeling annoyed, he put on a robe and went to open the door. Mr. Kárkányi, smiling, nodded that he wished to come in.

"Now?"

"Yes, please."

Javier opened the door and followed Kárkányi to the bathroom. The manager turned on the hot water-tap, waited a few minutes before putting his index and middle finger under the running water, and then asked Javier to do the same.

"Do you see what I mean, sir?"

It was hot, no doubt about it.

Now he wanted the help of that very same man. A petition he was contemplating with displeasure. He could ask the manager of another other hotel to get the information but then he'd have to change hotels. And that would be suspicious. The matter at hand was to ask Kárkányi to contact some thief or thieves. Hotel managers do business with all kinds of people.

He'd arrived at the museum, and in that gallery in particular, almost alone. After observing the viola di bordone for a long time, suspecting that it was a replica, a substitute, he finally convinced himself that he was standing before the instrument itself. Javier was able to press his ear against the glass case without the guards objecting, but also without being able to hear a single sound. He was filled with emotion. He returned on various occasions before it occurred to him to lift the glass case, shaped like a hollow cube missing one side, which covered the instrument. He wanted to touch the wood, the slackened strings, to see if that way he could hear the breathing. He managed to raise it a little, enough to insert three right fingers of his right hand, which remained trapped because the cube didn't budge any further and it turned out to be much heavier than Javier had anticipated. He saw the guard coming—he almost never made his rounds—and pulled his hand out violently. He managed to free it but he hurt his fingertips. He dried the sweat on his forehead with a handkerchief and now that the guard had again left, he brought his fingers to his mouth. He felt embarrassment. "This isn't work for an amateur," he thought, at the same time considering the possibility of committing a real crime. There were only two guards in the enormous pavilion, and the lack of security and the simple design of the vitrines—many of them empty—made him think that the most important thing to do in a robbery was to bribe the guard, or guards, on duty at night. He knew someone in the French Embassy who owed him a favor. As a diplomat, he could find a way to smuggle the viola out of the country. It was like adopting a child illegally. He surprised himself with these kinds of thoughts. The papers would have to be secured by a Jewish friend from Buenos Aires, a music lover as well as an antiquarian, someone who knew baroque and classical music like few others and was an *aficionado* of restoration. He did business in all kinds of instruments and could make that viola di bordone reappear legitimately from his store or workshop.

Now, seated in the chair, he thinks about how he'll broach the subject with the thieves. Perhaps the best plan would be for them to offer some money to the guards so they'd cover up the instrument's disappearance for an agreed upon period of time. Afterwards, he could ask them to return it to the place they'd taken it from. Javier would have already become familiar with the viola di bordone in a different manner and could listen to it in a future without feeling jealousy. Maybe not; maybe he'd never return it.

He keeps looking into the hall. He's gone down various times to the reception desk but he's only met the chambermaid. He's said to her, through gestures and facial expressions, that he'd like to see Mr. Kárkányi; that he should come up to his room as soon as possible. When he hears footsteps he thinks that the receptionist is coming up the stairs. But the steps belong to more than one person. There couldn't be fewer than two pairs of feet. It occurs to him that what's climbing the stairs are two actors disguised as a horse. Like in some comic opera. They don't use the elevator because it's very slow and it's almost always broken. He doesn't budge from the chair he's been sunk into for hours (except for brief trips to search for the manager). He approaches only with his gaze. Through the window, he's observed the sky darkening and the gradual but only partial illumination of the city. They don't knock. They walk past. He decides to look. He opens the door and sees the manager and two women in front of one of the other rooms.

The women are standing together, Kárkányi is to one side, to the left, slightly apart from them. As Javier observes them, they unbutton their coats. He sees their dresses, short and over the knee, made of combed cotton; the shoulder-straps reveal not only the necks of the two women, but also their shoulders and their upper bosoms. Their breastbones look like arches. Physically, they are twins; as far as their faces go, they look alike, although one's hair-color is dark and the other's is more red than blond. It would be hard to say which of them is lovelier or younger. They wear coats without really needing to on that summer night. They smile at him. Then they look at each other, which makes them both laugh, and Kárkányi's gaze passes from the young women to Javier and back to them. Javier feels a little out of breath. He looks at the floor. They're wearing black boots.

"Sophia speaks French," says Kárkányi, pointing to the brunette. He tells him in case Javier wishes such an arrangement in the future.

Javier no longer is listening to him. He returns to his room.

"Come in, come in, please," says a masculine voice, different from Kárkányi's. Then the two men, the guest and Kárkányi, begin arguing in French.

Javier lets a few minutes pass. When he goes to the door again, the hall is deserted. He feels a strange mix of fatigue and tension. He decides that he still can reach the museum before it closes.

He runs through the street. People watch him, a bit surprised. He doesn't want to take a taxi because the taxi drivers get lost on purpose so they can charge more. The museum closes at nine and it's only a few minutes before the hour. Although he arrives on time, the guards have already turned off the lights and he has to beg before they deign to let him enter, to turn on the lights—only in the corridor and in the exhibition gallery that interests Javier—and grant him ten minutes. They no longer bother accompanying him. They know him well. He walks alone through the corridor, the spotlights darkening behind him, and he arrives at the lit-up gallery.

He goes directly to the glass box. He gets so close that his breath clouds the glass. He leans over a little more, rests his right ear on the cold surface. His heart beats rapidly. He hears something that's growing stronger until its intensity makes him lift his head. He thinks it's the instrument. No, it's his own breathing, as if it were rebounding around him. He feels confused, dizzy, and rests his head once more on the glass box.

This time he hears nothing. It's Lilian whom he's been following! *And her breathing he's been listening to!* Has she also been looking for *him?* Although he's a man who almost never thinks about God, it occurs to him that now only God touches Lilian, and only Balázs Kakuk and various other mortals touch the viola di bordone.

Chanterelle

to Luis Fracchia and Rossana Durán

I see her, through the window, some distance away, on the other side of the pool, lying face-down on a towel, because her body is a different color than what I'm used to when I look toward that corner of the terrace every morning. Chanterelle has returned. In the months I've worked with Mr. Vogel, his daughter has appeared and disappeared half a dozen times. But I'd never really stared at her until this morning. I look at her obliquely, quickly, as I continue sitting down at the table, half of which is covered with mushrooms and fungi and the other with assorted books, a loupe, a towel, and a small knife. Mr. Vogel has classified most of them although he's left me as a task a small pile of those he still hasn't dared name, and another pile of mushrooms and fungi quite common to the region; I have to classify them using the tools at my disposal, including various books, some of them open. Mr. Vogel has great trust in those books, although what's most admirable, I think and smile at the thought, is that if you asked me how much I trust my employer's knowledge, I'd have to say not entirely but even so I eat the mushrooms and fungi he's selected to prepare his preserves, beef stews, and salads. He's a good cook, Mr. Vogel, he's spent years living alone, he knows only a few dishes but they're well-seasoned and I believe he enjoys cooking for me. In any event, we either eat food that he's prepared or each of us prepares his own, but he never eats what I've made. If in the first case, as far as trust, I seem to be a faithful or resigned servant, in the second case that can hardly be true since the man of the house prepares my meals and does it well, which is what I tell him, although he doesn't like praise. But returning to the table and the mushrooms, I believe that a true *connoisseur* would use his sense of smell above all. The knife and the loupe seem superfluous tools to me, unnecessary, objects for amateurs. When I made that comment to Mr. Vogel, he told me that he uses them in doubtful cases when he has to cut the soft, spongy flesh and observe close up the pigmentation or the little warts or moles. He added, pointing out that the need to explain himself annoyed and bored him, it's the tools that allow him to see details which, in turn, often distinguish an edible mushroom from a deadly poisonous one. Faced with such seriousness, I didn't say anything.

I've watched her movements since she got up from the side of the pool but I only look at her when she opens the glass door and goes inside; she walks toward the kitchen. She notices that I've seen her, but she doesn't return my gaze. We don't exchange a single greeting. I make as if to lower my eyes again to the mushrooms. She has long hair, a flaming red that I like very much, her pubic hair is the same color but with more yellow in it, bushy but perfectly outlined, she must shave it, and like a repetition of her pubic hair, although barely distinguishable, since she hasn't lifted her arms, I've seen the reddish hair of her armpits. She's passed by too quickly and the only thing that stays with me is this impression.

She comes out from behind the kitchen wall and again crosses toward the middle of the big room but then changes direction and moves toward the rear bathroom. This time I barely look at her. She's left the door open. She runs the water. I believe she's splashing her face. When she leaves she walks toward me or, actually, toward the sofa-bed, without my observing her, her lack of clothing doesn't let me really watch her, and she picks up something from the side of the bed and puts on her white panties, without sitting down, tugging gently with her hands, making a little hop, a lovely, childlike gesture, and when she bends again, I look at her back, and then her buttocks, thighs, the backs of her knees and calves, the soft white cloth, the skimpy cloth, lets me observe her and makes me tremble and standing up, she stretches her arms upward and slides them through the sleeves of her blouse until it covers her head. The first thing that emerges is her flaming-red hair and then with a gesture similar to the one she used to adjust her panties, she pulls her blouse down so that it finally covers her body as far as her waist. She raises her hands to her nape to free the long hair caught between her back and the cloth. She sits on the bed to finish dressing. It's the first time I've watched her like this. And she knows it.

Erik, the Swiss who sometimes works with me digging underneath the house because Mr. Vogel wants a basement and a wine-cellar, referred to Chanterelle in passing, immediately telling me about another one of his female friends, or better yet, about her tattoo: a cat that wraps around her right thigh, its rear paws near her sex, the cat's torso—along with its front paws, head and whiskers—on her buttock, in pursuit of a rodent that's disappeared, except for its tail, into the woman's anus.

"Herr Vogel wants his house to fall on top of us," he says and laughs, without stopping his hammering.

He's said that Chanterelle is beautiful, that she almost never visits her papa except during the summer, that she wanders from one university to another, that she feels more European than German and more German than Swiss, that she despises him as vulgar, that she almost never speaks, that just as I've seen, she walks around the house naked, like her papa does, that she's a redhead like Erik, and that it won't be long before she's gone.

"You're very quiet today," he says, without stopping his hammering.

Mr. Vogel hired him only to do this, to dig a pit under his house that in the future will be a *cava*, a wine-cellar. The rock is very hard, we make progress very slowly, Erik says that Mr. Vogel should rent an electric drill, he laughs and says that we look like *miserable* miners, that it's fine with him if the gentleman wants to flee civilization and build his house in the forest but to work like this seems to raise the cult of physical strength and manual labor to an absurd extreme.

He drinks from the two-liter beer bottle he always carries and offers me some. We're making little progress but in the seven weeks we've been working together we've opened a space big enough for an adult to fit lying down, although he might have to bend or crouch in order to enter or leave.

"This is a tomb," I say and Erik laughs.

He thinks that Mr. Vogel hasn't gotten the right tools for the job because I'm Mexican. I curse him in his own language, a Swiss-German dialect that he's been struggling to teach me. He tells me not to be offended. Besides, I wouldn't know how to use the equipment anyway, since it's obvious just by looking at me that the only heavy work I've done is what I'm trying to do as Mr. Vogel's employee. Erik keeps bringing up his strength and his knowledge of everything related to construction; in the time that I've spent talking to him—we see each other about twice a week to work on the cave, or grotto, although he started a few weeks before I arrived—he's paved most of the highways, opened most of the tunnels, and built several of the sluice-gates for the reservoirs in German Switzerland. He always concludes: *Now that's work*. The other kind, which is how he refers to jobs like Mr. Vogel's cellar, he does when he returns to his town, during his vacations, since he's traveled outside the country, to India, Greece, Morocco, but he doesn't enjoy it too much. Mr. Vogel is also worried that I might injure myself. That would have certain disastrous consequences: the high cost of my hospitalization, a lawsuit for hiring an illegal and his inevitable guilty conscience, since Mr. Vogel is a good man in all respects even if he hires illegals. I tell him that it's to keep down costs. You're wrong, he tells me, unskilled labor isn't cheap. He doesn't like drills, I add, for that reason he retired as a dentist. After so many years of drilling holes in his patients' molars, the last thing he wants is to bring that sound, even louder, into his house, and the idea of feeling those vibrations under his own feet must please him even less. You might be right, Erik says, this is a molar, and he picks up his hammer and chisel again. We work for a while without talking. The whole time I haven't stopped thinking about Mr. Vogel's daughter. It's a cavity, Erik says to me when we stop. He wipes the sweat from his brow and neck with his shirt, which he's taken off. He drinks some more beer and passes the bottle to me. "This will take a few months more and then we'll build the pool," he's right, I think, it was to build the pool that Mr. Vogel originally hired me. The one he has now is made of fiberglass, although that's disguised since it's sunken below the level of the wood-and-stone terrace, and surrounded by earth and containment walls. But that no longer satisfies him. As if thinking about him could make him materialize, Mr. Vogel appears, darkening the cavern, the grotto, the tomb, standing in the entranceway, his knees slightly bent, his body, too. Using phrases that sound mumbled and incomplete, he says something in German to Erik. He looks at me before turning and walking away, and with a wave of his hand, adds: *He'll tell you.* I've picked up my hammer and chisel again but Erik stops me. He's given us the rest of the day off, he says, which for him means that he'll be paid for eight hours but from this moment onward, I won't earn anything; I've gotten used to this, sometimes I feel like I've been invited, that I'm a guest in a small and comfortable, if somewhat rustic, hotel. The noise was bothering his daughter, he tells me, adding with a gesture that she's too delicate. "Herr Vogel told me that his daughter comes here to rest."

They offer us a lift in the back of a pick-up. We get off at the main square and choose the closest restaurant with a terrace, since after being stuck so long in a pit, we feel like sitting outside. We drink more beer and watch as a huge truck, which looks like it's carrying water or gasoline but is much bigger, moves toward the reservoir's sluice-gate. Erik explains that they're fish from Denmark, trout and salmon fry. They bring them from there to stock the lake. For sport-fishing, he says. It brings in a lot of money for the town. They come, I say, still amused, to a lake in the Swiss Alps for Danish fish. That's Switzerland, Erik says indifferently. Then he adds, with a guffaw: don't believe that the cows are from here. He winks and tells me that he thinks he wants to take advantage of the day to visit a little girlfriend, but before that, he talks for an hour and forty-three minutes about anarchism, which he considers himself a disciple of. He's worked side by side with internationally renowned anarchists, he gives

me their names but they don't mean anything to me, and he's
thinking of writing a book about the conversations he's had with
them. "Don't believe that they're any different from the one we're
having now, informal talks between comrades . . ."

"And what do *you* believe in," he asks me.

"I'm Catholic," I say, half-joking.

He becomes exasperated.

"Your politics, for God's sake!"

"I don't believe I have such beliefs."

"That's a good start," he tells me. "With time you'll know who
you are."

He must be four or five years older than me.

"Are you surprised that I'm an anarchist?" he asks, bragging.

"Yes, I have to admit, I imagined you more as one of the Pope's
Swiss guards."

He laughs. He begins to make a pyramid with the bottles
we've drunk, there are a lot of them and it's clear that he's done
this often, the sun is strong and my head hurts. Then a waitress
comes and takes away Erik's game, clicking her tongue, and I ask
her for the check. I tell Erik that I think I'll take a walk by the
lake and he says, She's cute, isn't she? And he continues looking
at the waitress as she walks away.

When I return to the house in the afternoon, I'm surprised to
see the sofa-bed folded up and not a single belonging of Chanterelle's anywhere. It isn't exactly like that: what surprises me
is noticing that she's gone and that I care. Mr. Vogel is seated
at the table in the big room. He's reading his newspaper but I
believe he's observed my reaction because he says: Chanterelle
will return, she left for a few days to visit her friends in Zurich,
and then he adds, a little annoyed, I think, at seeing himself give
explanations about his daughter's absence, that he's going out

and if I'm interested in earning some money tonight I can put the mushrooms and fungi now in the pot on the stove into jars, the way he's taught me. I'll have to wait until everything cools down. There are no longer any mushrooms on the table although Mr. Vogel points to those that he's taken care of separating, placing them on one of the chairs. Studying them now will help you the next time we go out, he says, and I don't contradict him, in spite of the fact that the first step, I suppose, on the agenda of a good mushroom collector is to find them, a skill I still don't possess. He gets up from the table and moves toward the stairs. I realize that he's been waiting for me. He comes downstairs again holding his jacket and car-keys. He won't return until tomorrow. We don't say goodbye. For Mr. Vogel, I think, saying goodbye and hello in the morning is unmanly.

I'm tense, nervous, a little frazzled and in spite of the fact that the idea of putting up the mushrooms feeds my lethargy, I know it's better to do it right away, besides, I'll earn some money, so I begin boiling the jars to sterilize them. The recipe is pinned to the wall above the kitchen table. As they boil, I look for the condiments on the different shelves and in the cupboard. I think that Mr. Vogel forgot to separate them but then it occurs to me that this is a sign of my employer's growing trust in me, which I'm grateful for, truly, I'm even happy for a while, everything is marked perfectly, as it should be, and the labels on the shelf match those on the little jars, but, as expected, everything is in German, so at times I have to open, try, smell, and compare to remove my doubts, which doesn't always happen, but I only use what I like. By now, the pot of mushrooms, and even more so its contents, is cool and using tongs I begin taking the jars out of the boiling water and placing them on a towel that I've spread over the kitchen table. The apron looks enormous on me because, like

62

almost everything else in this house, it belongs to the bear Vogel, that's what he's called by his nephew, the one who introduced us and got me the job, and I've also put on a cap to keep my hair in place. I'm becoming a German Swiss, I think. When the first round of jars is ready, I add the spices to them and, with special chef's tongs, place a generous selection of different kinds of mushrooms in each jar and then pour off a small amount of broth. After tightening the lid, I shake the jar gently so the leaves and spices are well-distributed, more or less. It's easier than doing the same thing with jars of preserves and blackberry jelly, which you have to fit with a wax stopper. I mustn't forget, I think, to tighten the lids in half an hour. I collect everything. I note the time; I've been working two hours and twenty minutes. I get the notebook and using a pen attached to it with a red ribbon, write down two hours and forty-five minutes. Out of superstition, or so I don't become discouraged, I've never figured out the total. When I work alone, I add ten percent since I don't take breaks; when I work with Erik I write down the exact time.

I've finished working but I don't feel any sense of satisfaction. I'm still restless. I walk through the big room and stop in front of the shelf with the collection of Mr. Vogel's pipes. I take down one of them, small and smooth, the wood and the black mouthpiece appeal to me. I snip off some leaves from the marijuana plant next to the window. They should really be used dry, I think, and it occurs to me to heat them up in a pan. Then I place the leaves, now more than dry, they're grilled, in the pipe and I go out to the terrace to smoke. I've removed leaves that Mr. Vogel won't notice are missing. When I finish smoking I come back inside, actually I haven't felt anything, maybe a little hunger, I have dinner, maybe I leave my hands under the hot water longer than usual when I wash the dishes, maybe the ham-and-cheese sandwich tasted better, the beer, too, maybe I feel more alone and can hear sounds more sharply from outside, wind through the branches. The moonlight on the pool seems like a sound at first and then an undulation though the water isn't moving, it could be coming from the clouds, the moon is behind the house so I can't see it. I go to the bathroom to brush my teeth but before I reach the sink, I stop to look at myself in the mirror, rather, the one who's in the mirror looks at me, which is why I stop. A clean-shaven face, suddenly with a mustache, then a beard, clean-shaven again, bald, normal, with a hat, a hat and mustache, I see out of the corner of my eye, beneath the mirror, a special shampoo for baldness and I laugh, I begin to make the changes happen by willing them, I realize that somehow *I'm* the one who's projecting these images in the mirror. Now the game includes clothing: I begin with something simple, a turtleneck sweater, I'm not aware of having wished for that color, it's black, then an overcoat, buttoned up at first, then open at the collar, then an overcoat and mustache, then a turtleneck and a bald head, then a smile and a mustache, then glasses and fedora and overcoat . . . I soon get bored, and I decide to finish doing what brought me here. As I brush my teeth, I think that because of my solitude, I'm becoming an idiot. The truth is that I didn't choose to work alone with Mr. Vogel. I wanted him to offer work to any one of my friends from the abandoned house in Gerosvil, I even told him to add up our hours and subtract a third of them. If you go to live with a hermit you become a hermit, I think and what comes to mind are the solitary men I've visited together with Mr. Vogel, most of them young, bearded and untalkative, dedicated to tending cows during the summer months, in the highest part of the Alps, near the glaciers. A man plus a hermit equals two hermits, I keep thinking. I understand why two men plus a hermit is a combination that might not interest Mr. Vogel. Soon we'd be seated around the pool, together with our Italian and Spanish friends. The solitary young men smoke pipes, I think, long, curved pipes, with decorations similar to what they put on cows, with metal lids and little silver chains, I believe, so the tobacco doesn't fall out as they work. They drink warm milk that tastes like grass. Where have I left the pipe? As I leave the bathroom, I feel thirsty, so I drink the last dregs from a beer bottle, eat some yogurt, and prepare a glass of cold chocolate milk, observing all the while that that combination normally disgusts me.

I climb upstairs and walk through the hall to the first of three bedrooms, near the stairs; it's the smallest and for now is being used as a service room. The rear bedroom belongs to the man of the house and the middle one is his daughter's, I suppose, although she prefers the sofa-bed. I head not to my own bed, to read and fall asleep, but to Mr. Vogel's bedroom and almost automatically, although I've resolved not to do it, I sit on the bed, leaning against the pillows, I take out the magazines from the dresser and leaf through them, looking once again at the faces, the bodies, the pubic hair, the genitalia I know so well that I can close my eyes during the day and remember them. I look through the pile of old magazines in the bottom drawer and find back-issues with images unfamiliar to me that, for this very reason, excite me even more. I place them around me. I look at the women on their hands and knees, thighs open, displaying their cunts and asses, their rounded buttocks, they look at whoever is looking at them—at the photographer, now at me, although I don't believe that they're actually looking at me—with their heads jerked upwards and doubled back over their own bodies. I've begun to masturbate and my sensitivity is even greater, I believe, because of the drug, but also sadness comes on quickly, which usually happens after I ejaculate, and now I feel it more strongly. I don't know what happens first—whether I stop masturbating or hear the sound of a vehicle approaching. I think it's Mr. Vogel. He must be entering the garage of his house. I pick up the magazines and put them away, trying to be careful, since Mr. Vogel is very observant, but I also act quickly—it doesn't escape me that I've gone from one kind of excitement to another—I arrange the bed, turn off the lamp, was it on or off when I came in?, and the pan, did I wash it? Did I tighten the lids of the jars? And the pipe? *The damned pipe!* . . . I remember that I haven't rinsed it out, or put it away, I don't even know where I left it. I go running downstairs, go out to the terrace, I don't find it, I don't dare turn on the light since Mr. Vogel could see me or may already have seen me because suddenly I'm surrounded by the glare of headlights, I enter and run through the big room, I run my hand over the little tables and the big one, the bookcase, the arms of the sofa and the sofa-bed, I don't find anything, I go into the kitchen, if Mr. Vogel walks in I'll pretend that I'm tightening the lids, I do it anyway as I look around the kitchen, without moving from where I'm standing, to see if I find the pipe, I go out to the terrace again, and in a moment that seems incredibly lucky to me, or one of great intuition, I take the pipe from one of the window-sills, without looking, more by touch than sight, and I pick it up a little bit frightened because I'm sure I didn't leave it there, but these aren't moments to distrust my own memory, much less trust it, so that I return running inside, I can't decide whether to enter the kitchen or climb the stairs, I decide that I don't have time to wash out the pipe and return it to its place; Mr. Vogel has already taken a long time, so I go upstairs, the smell of the pipe seems overpowering, an incriminating smell that's seeped into my hands, so instead of putting the pipe in its drawer, as I thought of doing, I open the little window in the room and feeling around the wall outside, I find a niche in the stone and place the pipe there and close the window again and keep quiet. The silence seems enormous to me and suddenly I realize that Mr. Vogel isn't going to arrive, that the car wasn't his, that I've imagined the beams of the headlights or they've come from some bend in the highway.

I should laugh at myself but I don't. I don't recover the pipe, either, so I can wash it and return it to its place. There are so many pipes that Mr. Vogel won't realize one is missing, he quit smoking more than ten years ago, he himself brags about it, those pipes are like a part of his past life, one ruled by leisure and marriage, I turn off the light and remember that my mother is always complaining that the servants move things around.

I sense that they're not here. Mr. Vogel's room doesn't reveal anything, everything is in its place, the bed made as always at this time. He gets up before I do and when I go downstairs he has breakfast prepared, or he's gone on ahead and is already swimming in his pool, or he's left me a note telling me what he wants me to do in his absence. When it's necessary for both of us to get up early for some task, he stands in the kitchen and bangs a huge metal spoon against a pan. I think he enjoys waking me up at the last minute to put pressure on me as I dress, I have breakfast and we leave the house. He enjoys this, he smiles at me as if to point out the joys of being an early riser. At night he goes to bed very early unless he leaves the house, which he also does early, before it gets dark, just bathed, with his long, thinning hair and his beard well combed, wearing clothes that while still informal, are clean and pressed. The irony doesn't escape me that I'm like a servant who wakes up after his masters. I don't hear any sound coming from below or detect any movement, looking from one side to the other of the enormous downstairs room that's used for everything: living room, dining room, library (with very few books).

A moment later I discover Mr. Vogel. He's cleaning the marijuana plant that caught my attention last night; he glides a half-lemon over each leaf. It's one of his favorites. He explains that it seems a little neglected lately. I look at him, look at the plant and then we both comment on its beauty before I go into the kitchen to make myself breakfast. Meanwhile, Mr. Vogel tightens the lids of the jars and then lifts one and holds it up against the light, inspecting it. He tells me that a lady friend has told him that marijuana preserved in alcohol is an excellent remedy for arthritis and rheumatism. He explains that he doesn't need such remedies but that he's thinking of increasing the number of his marijuana plants and including some kind of lotion among his products.

"It sounds like a good idea," I say.

"Besides," he tells me, "it's an excellent remedy for muscular pain."

As my first task he lets me finish cleaning the plant, and then he leaves the house. I do it with affection and then go into the kitchen and open the refrigerator to take out the eggs and cheese.

Mr. Vogel suddenly has the urge to assemble jigsaw puzzles, just like my paternal grandmother, I haven't told him that, maybe he wouldn't like the comparison, and he cares very little for the puzzle's theme, or image, as long as he can put it together and finish it quickly, like something irritating, without the patience or enjoyment my grandmother displayed, I haven't told him that either, but he does stay awake to put together puzzles and the next day he's in a bad mood, quieter than usual and more eager to do heavy labor like pulling out tree-trunks from the lake and

68

hauling them up the hillside to the house. On a few occasions, I took some pieces from the edges of the puzzle and returned them to the pile, after he'd gone to bed. It was never more than three, and I let a lot of time pass between one interference and another, always varying the number of pieces as well; the next day I arranged to sit exactly where I could watch his reaction. Mr. Vogel is almost childlike in the expressiveness of his gestures. I carried the joke too far one day when I decided to take one of the pieces from the edge and place it, not in the pile, but in the box next to my bed. He became infuriated. The first thing he did, knowing that he'd already found or seen it previously, was to look for only *that* piece, without success, and because of that he assembled the entire puzzle around the missing piece. Now I had no choice. I couldn't return the piece because it would expose me. I remarked that surely the manufacturer had forgotten to include *that* piece in the box. Mr. Vogel explained to me that such things don't happen in Germany. I suggested that maybe the previous owner had lost it. Mr. Vogel told me that there wasn't such an owner and that he himself had taken off the cellophane wrapping from the box. I buried the piece in the forest behind the house although I feared that it might show up, floating in the pool, or in the sink, or under some mushroom or on a raspberry bush, or stuck in a crack in one of the logs we pull from the reservoir, or stapled to one of the subscription forms in *Playboy* or *Penthouse*. Mr. Vogel finished the puzzle without finding the missing piece. He didn't return to his pastime for a few weeks. What began as a lighthearted, happy memory has become sad. I've let the omelet get cold and I stand up to warm it and toast the bread. The butter is a gift from one of my employer's clients and the blackberry jam that Mr. Vogel makes is extraordinary.

I think I hear water, as if someone were diving into the pool. After one of his daily walks or some job that he's preferred not to take me to, Mr. Vogel returns, passes through the gate to his garden and instead of walking on the stones set in the grass like huge tracks going toward the door, he dives into the water after taking off his clothes, crosses the small pool, gets out on the other side and enters the house through the glass door on the terrace without drying himself off, stops in the middle of the big room, suddenly standing in shadow with water running down his whole body, as if he didn't know how to make use of the remaining hours in the day. I look into the big room and, in effect, there's Mr. Vogel, although now he's turned and walks toward the stairs, which is also his usual pattern. He'll go upstairs to his room and rest there for half an hour or forty minutes, maybe wrapped in a big towel, maybe reading, maybe asleep. I collect everything from the table, put back whatever belongs in the refrigerator, wash the dishes, wipe down the counters with a wet rag, and throw out the trash, tossing part of it into the bin for organic material, and the rest in three containers marked *glass, paper and cardboard,* and *metals and plastics.*

In response to my indirect question regarding the length and frequency of his daughter's visits, Mr. Vogel tells me that he never knows. That there's no way of knowing whether or not she'll return soon.

She returns. On her own. I don't know at what moment she crosses the last tunnel before entering the long, narrow valley, I don't notice her flaming-red hair rising toward me along the highway although the roof of the car hides it from view, her smell doesn't waft toward me like the smell of bread that Mr. Vogel bakes. After days in which she's appeared before me repeatedly, when I least expect it, as I'm breaking the rock under the house, as I'm peeling a garlic clove to make myself spaghetti, as I'm walking behind Mr. Vogel on a path high in the mountains, without ever going by unnoticed, I now go downstairs and see her seated in the big room. She's reading, the lamplight falls above her tilted head and shoulders like a lighter shade of her hair-color. She acknowledges my presence with a glance. I greet her the same way. I sit down at the table facing Mr. Vogel since he's invited me to play *gin-rummy*. He offers me a schnapps. Its color, just like the lamplight, is an alternate shade of Chanterelle's hair. It's raspberry, Mr. Vogel tells me and I remember the reddish mat of hair with a touch of yellow, clipped and slightly bushy, over Chanterelle's pubis. Her father looks at me impatiently since my gaze isn't focused on the cards or on the table but, I imagine, into space. We read, or should I say Chanterelle reads, for a long time, and we end up with Mr. Vogel ahead one hundred points and me with almost none. He suggests raising the ante to 200 and, in a magnanimous gesture, glancing from the corner of his eye at his daughter so that she knows of his crushing victory as well as his generosity toward a defeated enemy, he offers me a clean slate and another round. I smile at him. As many as he wants, as long as his daughter is here and I can observe her, absorbed in reading, or at least pretending to, with the subtle play of emotions showing on her face, in the movement of her lips, in the opening and closing of her eyes, in the tilt of her head to one side or forward, in the way she adjusts her body in her chair. She doesn't stop or raise or lower the book, although she raises her knees to rest her forearms on them, showing part of her thighs underneath the long, Indian skirt with geometric patterns and lively colors, a little faded, maybe from use, from numerous washings in some Parisian laundromat; I imagine Chanterelle facing the clothes, with numerous folds and a soft appearance, turning around and around. Afraid that Mr. Vogel will see me, I stare at her thighs, looking for her panties, which I imagine are made of another kind of cloth and texture, and her sex, which is covered and seems to be breathing through the cotton. I imagine Chanterelle within a few months. She walks out of what looks like a university building into the cold street, rubbing herself as she exhales the warm air, the smell of wet wool and her own breath and saliva gathering in the light, damp cloth of her scarf.

In a little while she informs us, pretty and drowsy, that she's going to sleep, and I hope that her father invites her, insists that she eat dinner with us, but Mr. Vogel, without breaking out of his usual silence, says nothing, he looks at me a little impatiently again because once more I've forgotten that we're in the middle of another hand of *gin-rummy*. As she passes, I say: "Wouldn't you like to have something for dinner?" She responds: "No, I almost never eat dinner," and then, after a silence in which she pauses before leaving, she says "Thank you." She says it in German. I observe the way she walks to the sofa-bed. I believe that her father is also observing her. Our game loses the tension granted by Chanterelle's closeness. Out of the five hands, I win two and after a while we get bored. We go into the kitchen to prepare something for dinner and turn out all the lights except one so we won't disturb Mr. Vogel's daughter who has already lain down and turned off the light next to her bed.

I sleep badly. I ask myself if she goes to bed the same way she walks around the house. I imagine myself at the foot of her sofa-bed, lifting the sheet to kiss one of her ankles, then the other, placing myself under the sheet to continue kissing her legs, from one to the other, zig-zagging to her sex. My lapping tongue opens her up and, in my imagination, at that moment she asks me to come into her arms and penetrate her. Even better, I imagine that she comes upstairs and pulls back the curtain to my room. She's wearing white panties and a black slip and her coloring has never seemed more extraordinary. I sit up in bed, sit on the edge with my feet on the floor and she approaches, her abdomen almost level with my face, explaining that this bedroom was always hers, that this is where she slept when her father built the house and she was still a little girl, that this is where she slept last summer, that this is where she always slept when she visited her father, that the room next to it was her brother's. I begin to get up to give her the bed, that's the right thing to do, I'll sleep on the sofa but she takes me by the shoulder and pushes me so I'll sit down again and comes even closer and there's a tense moment; I press my face against her belly and grab her buttocks. When I start putting my fingers beneath the cloth and she opens her legs a little, I know that she's not there, but downstairs, I think about going downstairs, I know I won't do it, but I walk toward the bathroom at the end of the hall. I've turned on the light beside my bed, I've walked close to the banister so I'll be easily seen, I've opened and closed the door noisily. I want them to hear me, to know that I'm awake, that I've entered the bathroom. Actually, I don't have to go, it occurs to me it might have been better to go down to the kitchen for a glass of water, that way I'd be closer to her.

I turn off the faucet I'd turned on for no other reason than to be consistent, to achieve certain sound effects. It occurs to me that Mr. Vogel is listening to me, that he's paying attention to the sounds. Could he be asking himself about my intentions, imagining that I like his daughter? And is Chanterelle also listening to me? I keep quiet for a while, without turning off the light, then I turn it off as if I'd already gone, maybe it might occur to Chanterelle to use the bathroom because she's heard me, a sympathetic movement, but there's no noise, I turn on the light again, turn on the faucet, wet my face, dry it, look at myself in the mirror and it occurs to me that Chanterelle is asleep and if she happened to hear any of the noise I was making, it would only annoy her. She must be about twenty-five years old. I smile at myself in the mirror. I look at myself a long time, with every instant a feeling of utter stupidity builds inside me and I don't have the courage to go into the kitchen for a glass of water or return to my room and go to sleep.

I wake up and when I realize I'm the only one in the house, I curse myself for hardly ever getting up early. When Chanterelle is here, she becomes her father's companion. Mr. Vogel has left me a note. I read it. Erik won't come today but I can do whatever I want on the *cava* job.

As always, it's hot, it's a small, tight space, even more so because of the physical labor, but I feel at home. I mark a certain point on the rock that I should reach in a half-hour, in an hour, I check to see if I've been able to loosen a certain amount of the rock, the work will distract me from thinking, the hammering is a sound that pleases me, my sweat pleases me, I've taken off my shirt, it pleases me to feel stronger and more agile than when I began months ago. I stop working after three hours and walk over to the little table in the big room, still not putting on my shirt, and I write down *three hours* in the notebook and think that this time I've done a good job for my employer, that I've done a lot of work considering what I'll be receiving in Swiss francs. It occurs to me to go for a swim; not in the reservoir (where I sometimes remove logs, although my employer insists that I shouldn't do it, that it's dangerous; Erik thinks Mr. Vogel's only concern is his fear of finding himself accompanying an undocumented worker, wounded or drowned, to the hospital) but in his pool, where he hasn't prohibited me from swimming but he hasn't invited me to do so, either. Of course, I haven't seen them swimming during Chanterelle's visits, either, or sat by the edge of the pool, or looked at them from the glass door, or done any work in areas bordering the pool. I've seen them the way servants watch their masters conduct certain activities, as they enter the big room, on this occasion, naked, as I exit after them, now that the water is calm and the moisture on the stone has dried. The opposite isn't true, either: I don't hold up a towel, standing at a respectful distance, for them to take from my hands, although now it occurs to me that I would love to do that for Chanterelle and see her reaction, of surprise, haughtiness, or laughter. Mr. Vogel swims to wash off his sweat, to refresh himself, he doesn't like to do many laps in the pool, he swims just a little, for a short while, he does his exercise on his walks and I don't believe he really likes getting wet. Chanterelle, on the other hand, really enjoys it. She stays in the water longer, I hear her splashes, she suns herself lying on the stone.

I'm going to swim, I think, and I begin to undress. When I'm in my underwear, I decide that I won't swim naked. I place my clothes on the arm of Chanterelle's sofa-bed. I poke around in a box full of old clothes that Mr. Vogel has pointed out and told me I could use for heavy work or just because I like some of the garments, and I find the shorts I've seen before. Their youthful cut makes me doubt that they're his. They're a little big on me so I tie them with a cord I take from one of the drawers in the kitchen. I enter the water at one end, sliding in silently and trying not to break the glassy surface. The water feels cold, more so because of my body-heat. Now immersed, I feel immense pleasure and I swim at the deep end, near the bottom, holding my breath as I go from one side to the other, turning, pushing off with my feet to return. I feel an extraordinary freedom, an expansion through my skin and my sight. I rise to the surface and turn over, face-up, to take a breath, trying to surface as little as possible, and I sink again, exhaling, watching how the bubbles rise toward the surface, until I'm first sitting, then lying down on the bottom of the pool, with my lungs almost empty. I play like that. The house, apparently alone, is surrounded by other houses, by eyes, voices, gossip that I've heard about others and about myself that has reached me indirectly. I don't want anyone to know that I'm swimming in Mr. Vogel's pool; the sensation of doing something in secret also pleases me, moving in a medium that isn't my own but that agrees with me, keeping a silence that doesn't contradict but invigorates my movements, my displacements, everything I do under the surface, somehow hidden except for those who approach and draw away, keeping the surface almost smooth as if nothing were happening. I get out but don't lie in the sun, I don't recline on the plastic chaise, either, or leave the shape of my body on the wet stone, although I do leave the shape of my soles there, or use the beach-towels. I take a hot shower, I dress, I hang the shorts from the window of my room, on the way recovering the pipe I'd lost, but then it occurs to me that the red-and-yellow shorts might look like a flag to anyone approaching this side of the house, so I take them down, rinse out the pipe, place it where it belongs, put the shorts with my other dirty clothes in the washing-machine (it's the first time I've done this but I'll explain to Mr. Vogel that it was necessary to use it since I haven't gone to Gerosvil in a few weeks). I go out and walk along a wide dirt path, so I can get some sun and also feel against my boot-soles the heat rising from the ground. I go down toward the lake and take a walk for half an hour at a leisurely pace.

In the afternoon I prepare lasagna, with ground meat, mushrooms, ham, cheese, and fresh tomatoes, I think about Chanterelle, I imagine her entering at the moment the smell of the lasagna, now in the oven, begins to fill the house. Yes, she'll accept what I've prepared to eat and when he sees her accept, maybe Vogel the bear will also deign to try something. It's a pity I didn't stop in town for a bottle of good red wine, I think, but they don't arrive, I turn off the oven so that the pasta doesn't dry out, I serve myself a glass of beer, I take out the lasagna, it seems a little dry to me, I moisten it with some beer from the bottle, I wait a good while, I walk to the glass door, at one point going out to the stone path, I return, I finish heating the pasta, they still don't arrive, I decide to eat, I have it with garlic bread and salad, the dressing is made of apple vinegar and olive oil, they still don't arrive, I serve myself another portion, I'm surprised at the size of my appetite, I open another bottle of beer, I eat, I clean the plate with the bread, I take another very small portion of lasagna with my fork, I think that now I shouldn't eat any more and then it occurs to me that what's left in the glass dish must be enough for both of them, otherwise they'll prepare their own food. The idea worries me, after what I've eaten, will there be enough for both of them? I make a calculation and draw imaginary lines with my knife over what remains and decide that they're rather small portions and I don't want to seem ungenerous. They still haven't arrived so I serve myself another portion. When I finish eating, I put in the refrigerator the leftover lasagna, which has now gotten cold, a good-sized portion for one person but not for two, it's like beds, I think, the portion is more like a single bed. I wash the dishes, I prepare coffee and I drink it with a piece of bittersweet chocolate. They still might arrive, I think. We could drink a cup of coffee together, in case they've already eaten, which is more likely considering the time. Mr. Vogel could offer us a glass of his raspberry schnapps. I think again about Chanterelle's coloring. Actually I haven't focused on her skin, on the color and shape of her nipples, on whether or not she has freckles (redheads usually do) and on what parts of her body. I haven't touched her. I don't know what she smells like, either. I've hardly heard her speak, I don't know her laugh, I'd like to hear her when she's angry or whispering something to someone, or singing when she thinks she's alone. She hasn't arrived and I feel very frustrated. I decide to lie down and sleep. I lie down but I don't sleep, I see the time and it occurs to me that although it's early the day has seemed too long to me, I've worked only three hours and that isn't much money. Besides, working will let me accomplish what I might have gained with sleep, so I go out to the garden with that hope and start moving rocks from one spot, where the truck left them, to another, near where the future pool will be, work without mythical resonance since the ground is flat and the stones aren't enormous but the size of a bowling ball. It isn't one of the jobs that most interests Mr. Vogel but the idea of returning to the cave doesn't appeal to me, and now that he's disappeared (together with his daughter) without making it clear what he expects of me, except to wait for him and, since the one I'm really waiting for is his daughter, I apply myself to moving stones, counting them at first, then counting the number of steps from one pile to another. It's an activity I've done very few times over the summer; it occupies the second-to-last place on my list of potential chores and projects that Mr. Vogel handed me the second morning after I arrived at his house in the country. I work two hours, until I feel pain in my lower back and neck. Mr. Vogel's house has never seemed less my home, in spite of being small it takes up an enormous amount of space that no matter what I might wish, is impossible to fill.

They arrive and I wake up enough to know it's them and that they're speaking in German, and I fall asleep again almost immediately, no longer feeling any anger, but, yes, feeling a certain apparent indifference that grants me a pleasurable sense of power, short-lived since in the morning the first thing I do is make an appearance. I see her sleeping on the sofa-bed and go downstairs, wearing a robe I've seen in the bathroom that Mr. Vogel has told me I can use, to the kitchen to prepare myself a cup of coffee. I use my Italian espresso-maker and almost the last of the coffee I bought on my visit to Geneva. If I wasn't successful with the lasagna, I'm now confident I can offer Chanterelle a cup of coffee. When the aroma has completely filled the kitchen, I appear in the big room. Chanterelle is seated in bed, still under the sheets, her knees raised, hands crossed in her lap and her body leaning against the backrest.

"Would you like a cup of coffee?" I ask her in French.

"Yes," she says.

"With cream and sugar?"

"Just a little cream."

"O. K."

I disappear and return with the cup and hand it to her. She tries it.

"It's delicious."

She puts the cup on the little table next to her bed.

"And you?" she asks me. "Aren't you going to have a cup?"

"I already had one," I lie. The last thing I want to do right now is walk away, although I reflect that maybe going for a cup might have made it possible to spend more time with her. I look around discreetly, I believe, and she notices it and without inviting me to sit on her bed tells me why don't I pull up a chair. I do so and then we talk about the coffee and she says that although what I've prepared is exquisite, generally she prefers it Turkish-style. The conversation lasts the time it takes her to drink her coffee, a few small sips, just a moment but I enjoy it, and even more her gesture when she's finished. She tells me that along with coffee, or fresh orange juice, the most agreeable way to wake up is to go for a swim. She sits at the edge of the bed, her back to me, she gets up and loosening the straps of her nightgown she lets the garment fall over her shoulders to the floor and walks toward the glass door. I don't know whether to leap up and open it so she won't have to exert herself or to go look for oranges in town although the ones I've tried are from Israel and are tasteless. I don't do either, I watch her until she's dived head-first into the water.

I return to the kitchen. I drink my coffee. I leave her cup so she won't forget our moment together, so she'll think about me when she sees it. I don't have breakfast now since before watching his daughter and talking with her, I read a note that Mr. Vogel left for me on the table. In it he asked me to carry the two bags of preserves to town and to deliver them to Frau Helda. I go upstairs to get dressed. I'll eat breakfast later, I think.

When I return to the house—it occurs to me that my main activities in those days were going and coming—I walk on the stones set in the ground and see that Chanterelle is next to the pool, sunning herself and reading a book. I prefer for her not to see me, or to ignore me, than to greet me as if it were an obligation, with a rapid and slightly annoying movement of her hand, or by raising and lowering her book or tilting her head. Her serenity suits her well, I think. I don't offer her breakfast because I've already had something to eat in town, and because tomorrow I'll again bring her coffee in bed but that doesn't mean I feel like going out to the terrace to ask what she might like for lunch. Mr. Vogel isn't in the house. I sit at the big table with all the mushrooms and fungi. I begin to study them, it's a task I now enjoy, I've become quite attached to them, underneath the earth, barely peeking out, in the niche of an old tree, on the table, in Mr. Vogel's stews, in pots or jars, in the bag I've taken to Helda this morning. I notice Chanterelle when she's already beside me. She's naked, her skin warm and flushed, with drops of sweat on her forehead, just below her hairline.

"My father keeps classifying mushrooms," she says and her comment is neither an affirmation nor a question.

"Yes," I tell her.

She picks up one of the mushrooms. Me, seated at Mr. Vogel's table at his house in the country, and Chanterelle on her feet, gently leaning against the edge, looking at me, and what I remember isn't the mushroom in her hands, but the way she was looking at me. It was the same as her smile, sweet and sad, barely suggested, a little shy, although also as if she were waiting for something, her question is blunt but not lacking in sweetness.

"What's it called?"

I observe the mushroom, which lets me watch the skin of Chanterelle's shoulder and neck. I reach for a book that's about a meter away and consult it. I go back to studying the mushroom, this time watching her breasts and nipples among the many

81

branches, which are smooth with edges like little teeth made of white flesh, at times yellowish or gray along those edges. I read: firm with a pleasant odor; the spore's design: white; the spore: ovoid, colorless, smooth. I run my finger down the page until I reach its name.

"Clavulina cristata," I say to Chanterelle.

She puts down the Clavulina cristata and picks up another. "And this?"

I recognize it immediately but I want to prolong the game, so I start leafing through the *Concise Illustrated Book of Mushrooms and Other Fungi*, looking repeatedly at the specimen that Chanterelle holds up, this time not in one hand but in both, which gives her breasts another shape.

I read the description out loud.

"And is it edible?" she asks and I continue thinking about what I've just read, the gills extending downward along the stalk, not too deep, like loosely-spaced pleats that form interconnected branches; the stalk two-to-five centimeters thick, short, getting thinner toward the base, which is often almost flattened, smooth; the slender flesh soft but firm, with a pleasant smell of dried apricots. . . .

"Yes, it's excellent to eat."

Chanterelle has freckles on the upper part of her torso, between her breasts and the base of her neck. I consult the book again.

"They recommend drying it in the sun or cooking it fresh, on a low flame with butter."

"Very interesting," she says, a little bored, and puts down the mushroom.

"It's not easy to find," I read, in order to say something, to hold back Chanterelle, who wasn't named that but now as I write this, I can't remember her real name. "It can be confused with the false Chanterelle (*Hygrophoropsis aurantiaca*), which is more common, and which is found in coniferous forests. Another related species is the autumnal Chanterelle (*Cantharellus tubaeformis*)."

I'm startled when I turn around and see Mr. Vogel standing by the kitchen doorframe. I don't know how long he's been there listening to us. His daughter looks at him nonchalantly and tells him something in German. Both of them laugh. Mr. Vogel says that we have to work to do. That I should put on my pants and boots since we'll be climbing to one of the cabins in the Alps. I say goodbye to Chanterelle with a wink.

"We'll continue the lesson later," I tell her in French.

"I don't think so," she says. She already knows we won't see each other again. She adds: "All the best to you."

I think that she's referring to the work her father has summoned me to do.

"Thanks," I tell her and she smiles. Maybe she thinks that her father has already told me about her departure. I go upstairs to change and when I return Chanterelle and her father are standing on the terrace. They say something and then she walks toward the pool, this time without turning around, bare from the soles of her feet to her makeshift bun, and Mr. Vogel approaches me and with a gesture directs me to follow him. We leave through the wooden gate to a path in the forest behind the house that takes us to a trail bordering the Alps along the valley. I will woo her, I tell myself. From the beginning of our walk I'm already thinking about our return. About what I'll say to her. About inviting her to play some table-game, or to drink a beer in town. I feel excited, an emotion that will keep on growing throughout the day. We walk along the high, narrow trail and open the metal gate to enter and then close it.

"For the goats," Mr. Vogel explains to me for the umpteenth time.

It doesn't fail to amaze me that there's a faucet in that spot; we drink water to refresh ourselves and splash our faces.

There are two tasks. I help out with the first one: to repair three broken windows. Mr. Vogel asks me if I'm interested in helping with the second one: to slaughter a pig. The animal's owner looks at me. I tell him that unless my help is indispensable, I prefer not to do it. The two men move toward the pigsty. I walk toward the mountain-side. I quickly cover a good distance since I don't want to hear the screams. I climb onto a big rock and sit in the sun. I decide at that moment to stop eating meat. My unwillingness to slaughter animals should also make me avoid slaughtered meat. It's not the first time I've had this thought. I've been reading a study on Buddhism. The decision makes me feel happier. I return when I hear Mr. Vogel shout my name. I enter and see that they're hanging up the rubber aprons, now washed, on a hook. I realize that I haven't heard anything, which doesn't take away the gloominess of what's just happened here. It's beyond me how Mr. Vogel ended up practicing all these different trades.

We return, both of us happy, we descend in a hurry, we cross paths with a ram whose appearance and bad smell make us laugh.

"One of those is enough for two hundred females," Mr. Vogel informs me. "They can smell him over the whole area."

The animal looks at us. Actually, it's beautiful. Three times bigger than the females, with long dark brown and black fur, a white tuft on its chest and one between its horns, and very peculiar eyes—almost horizontal black bands against a gold background. We stop in a few places, where we haven't been in a few weeks, to look for mushrooms. I'm having a good time, as usual, without making any great discoveries, but Mr. Vogel celebrates each one of his finds with a little shout. As I poke among the leaves and loose, wet earth, I think that next time Chanterelle will set aside the mushrooms and fungi and lie down, first face-up, then face-down, and invite me to search her for the most likely places to find mushrooms. They grow in slightly moist places, in the shade or almost in darkness, in slightly acidic earth, covered with leaves, next to a tree-trunk. She'll invite me to lie down gently, telling me to practice on her whatever's necessary to recognize what I'm now looking for under the huge trees in the forest where we've descended. I'm thinking about this when Mr. Vogel shouts that we should return to the house. I go ahead, running like crazy down the mountain, now through the pastures where the cows look at me or move back several steps, making their bells clang when I slap them on the back. I laugh, I take a few leaps that seem superhuman to me, I remember a similar moment when, alone in my employer's house, I watched dusk fall over the lake and between the hills, so beautiful I started to sing, to emit sounds that seemed strange but at the same time completely natural, a gamut of notes I discovered at that moment, high and sustained, I thought, I didn't really know where I was and, as it became dark, I fell silent. I wait for Mr. Vogel to enter the house. I prefer it that way, to calm down a little, catch my breath. When I enter, it immediately hits me that Chanterelle has gone. It's Sunday afternoon.

"Your daughter?" I ask my employer.

He makes a gesture that means he doesn't really know, but that her disappearance doesn't surprise him. I say that I'm going to take a shower. He gets undressed to take a dip in the pool. The afternoons are now cool. Summer is ending and fall is beginning.

I cry in the shower and decide I'll leave as planned, on Wednesday, in three days' time.

The days are silent, sad for both of us, I believe; a strange comradeship grows between us, which at first I explain as the result of Chanterelle's departure, but later also seems related to the fact that in a few days I'll be leaving too. Mr. Vogel will have no company. We do the things we like best, pulling out tree-trunks from the reservoir, looking for blackberries, preparing and putting up the last jams of the summer. One morning Erik arrives and Mr. Vogel tells him to return the following week. We say goodbye to each other. He promises to look me up in Spain on his next trip out of Switzerland.

The day Mr. Vogel takes me to the bus-stop it occurs to me that I haven't climbed into his car since the time he picked me up. We've eaten well, Mr. Vogel has accepted the coffee I've prepared and the coffee-pot as a gift, he's paid me generously, calculating all the quarter-hours as full hours. He hands me a thick wad of bills, a lot of money in Spain, and I thank him for the money, the job, and the summer in his house. Along the road, we barely talk. He asks me what I'm studying in Spain. I tell him theology. He thinks that theology is very dry.

I take a lot of the things I've borrowed these last months from the box of clothes—a pair of rubber boots, a few shirts, a pair of woolen pants, all too big on me but too small for him—and I don't know how many of them are really mine, and how many he's given me as gifts, or only meant for me to use when I was with him. It's gotten dark along the way and when we arrive at the bus-stop, Mr. Vogel says he'll wait for the bus to come so I don't have to get out. It's begun to drizzle and it's getting cold. I tell him not to bother, that it's better for him to return to his house in case the rain gets worse, I point out that the stop has a roof and that I'll be fine. I say goodbye, and he takes my hand in a strong, slightly lingering, handshake to mask the overpowering emotion we both suddenly feel. The reservoir is behind me. From where I'm standing, I can see the tunnel that will take me out of the valley again.

The Midnight Man

to Joby and Beth Taylor

"When did you know that he liked you?" Ana asked her.

He'd looked at her legs. Paula was wearing jeans and black-and-white sneakers. Lem adjusted himself in his seat and stretched his legs so he could see if they reached the imaginary pedals on his side of the car. He looked at Paula's legs again, from the white laces to her waist.

Paula drove fast and ably, her body thrust backward, both hands on the steering-wheel. Her posture was relaxed and at the same time alert.

"I really like your legs," Lem said. "They're so long. They're a little like a teenage boy's."

"Do you like teenage boys?" Paula asked him.

"No," said Lem, "but I like the way you resemble a teenage boy. I could watch you from the waist down from here till the hotel. I'd like to see you in a skirt or shorts. Although the sneakers look nice on you."

When they arrived at the hotel, he invited her to go upstairs with him to smoke pot. She could relax that way, she could let go and talk about herself.

"Maybe another time," Paula said as a good-bye.

The New Yorker was curious about her house, he told her, as if this, the objects and spaces that surrounded Paula, would help him convince her to shift from their professional life, as friends, as she put it, to something else. He got her address from the newspaper office and arrived without warning. Paula was at the movies with her cousin. When the servant brought him into the living room and from there went to Don Rodolfo's studio to advise him that someone was looking for his daughter, Lem wanted to run away.

"You have an appointment with my daughter?"

"That's right. I wanted to show her some of the results from work."

"Did you bring them with you?"

"No. I thought I'd return to the studio with her."

"What a pity, I would have liked to see them." My daughter has told me a lot about you. I don't know where she is but she shouldn't be much longer. She's not forgetful."

They talked about New York and Mexico City. Then Lem, who'd traveled over the world even more than Sr. Neira, told him about some of his experiences as a photographer. Whenever the host recognized any of the places mentioned, he'd add comments and anecdotes. They seemed to be comfortable but Paula didn't arrive and Sr. Neira offered him a drink.

Paula was in the house, but locked in her bedroom. That's what the New Yorker felt and told her afterwards. His trips around the world had allowed him to meet many people, and though he knew it would be highly unlikely for Sr. Neira to be rude to him, his first visit to her parents' house would also be his last. He studied some of Sr. Neira's gestures and features and saw his daughter reflected in them.

Some photos from one of the albums on the coffee table disappeared. They were family photos. Surely Lem had leafed through them while waiting for the gentleman's return. Ana and Paula laughed and then Ana wanted to know which they'd been and laughed even more when she learned there was one of Paula in a bikini in the first album. She must have been about sixteen and was standing next to a man disguised as a pirate on some Acapulco beach. There was a whole sequence, beginning when Paula was eight. The same pirate, each time older, was her partner at different times, at eight years, at nine, at thirteen, at fifteen and in the last, which Lem had decided to take for himself. He'd left the others in the album on the coffee table.

Sr. Neira still wouldn't reappear. Lem would start leafing through another album. Normally he wasn't a kleptomaniac, Paula supposed. In that other photo she must have been eleven or twelve—it was one of her favorites—even-tempered and regal in her bearing, dressed as a ballerina, a witch, a queen, an Indian, a bird?, she held her parents by the hand and seemed to be taking care of them. She'd taken the trip to the Carnival with them when she'd turned twelve.

Lem had pulled out that photo and various others from the album, leaving blank squares, with a date above the place each image had occupied.

"He's crazy, Ana said. "Have you asked him to return them?"

"No, imagine! It's better if he keeps them."

She told Ana about that night in the Plaza de San Pedro. It had been full of people. The paper streamers as if from some gigantic multicolored spider-web covered everyone, the band waiting on the stage, the prostitutes on the side-street, the coffee vendors with their wooden boxes, opening and closing the lids to the rhythm of *forró*, the shirtless men sweating, the women in tight clothes, their hair covered with scarves to protect it from the talc. If the image was of a spider-web, the movement of everyone was like waves that begin in the center of a body of water and radiate slowly toward the shore. *Si você não conhece o carnival de Recife, não conhece Recife, quarto dias de amor. O melhor carnival . . .**

The man's stomach revolted, staining the suit he'd paid for so dearly; one could hear the prostitute's screams as she was carried through the alley, kept on her feet and kicked by three military police officers in green uniforms and white helmets so that she kept walking; they were followed closely by an official dressed in blue. The Danzantes de Maracatú, exhausted, were seated on the curb, sad, as if the spectacle had drained them not only physically, but also in spirit, while a singer with a microphone, drums, and an audience around him was observed, among others, by a drunk or crazy man who was also singing, imitating him, until a boy pulled him by the pant-leg and then ran behind a post, unable to stop laughing. There was also something grotesque or simply a little ridiculous about the two civilian policemen, dressed very smartly, pacing back and forth, suddenly guarding an empty plaza instead of a lively crowd.

Everyone had left and only Paula and her parents remained in the restaurant and, outside, through the windows, the group of men seated in a corner of the plaza, now empty and silent except for the voices that responded to an old man who strummed a guitar and sang about hunger in the Northeast, the hard life of the Sertão, droughts, love, a betrayal, politics . . . their voices filled the plaza, just like their hats, which seemed to have a life

---

*If you don't know the Recife carnival, you don't know Recife, four days of love. It's the best carnival . . . [trans.]

of their own, responding to the man and then falling silent and listening to him.

"Now it's very late for a certain *señorita*," her father had said, breaking the enchantment.

The man of the house returned.

That's what Lem told her.

"All we can do is wait," Sr. Neira said, handing him his drink.

They sipped their whiskeys for a while.

Paula and Ana played at recreating the dialogue.

"That over there isn't a dog," Sr. Neira would say, pointing to the toy dog that had entered from the kitchen and now was in Lem's lap. "Dora doesn't let me have a real dog because it would finish off this one. And I'm not referring to its size. I like bulldogs very much, and a bulldog would toss Chu Chu into the air as if he were a rat and then he'd break his back. Do you like dogs?"

"I prefer cats."

"I should have known."

Gazing at Chu Chu with a look that combined the *connoisseur* with the snob, Don Rodolfo would begin talking about all the dogs he'd had, their names, breeds, pedigrees, and personalities, likes and gestures, in short, he'd talk about them with greater gusto, knowledge and affection than about his own family.

They would have another whiskey.

"I'm sorry, but I should go."

"Wouldn't you like to have dinner with us?"

"No, thanks very much. Maybe another time," Lem would say, glancing at his watch to make it understood he had another appointment.

"I'm sorry, I don't know what's happened with the young lady. We taught her to be punctual."

"Don't worry. It was a pleasure meeting you."

Sr. Neira would walk him to the door.

Lem returned to his hotel room (this he did tell Paula) where he continued drinking whiskey, but with tap-water and not on the rocks.

"Your photographer friend is unbearable," her father told her when Paula returned from the movies. "Boring the way only gringos can be. He talked to me the whole time about his travels. The poor guy doesn't know what it means to stay in one place longer than a month. He seems more like a stewardess or a *traveling salesman* than a photographer."

"Have you noticed that rich people talk about their dogs and poor people about their children?" the New Yorker asked Paula the next time they saw each other, again at the Santa Fe garbage dump.

The permit from the Álvaro Obregón police station had cost the New Yorker fifty dollars in bribes and having to listen to a long discourse on the dignity of the people who work in the Santa Fe garbage dumps, and he'd counted on spending a hundred dollars at most to enter as far as the part of the dump that interested him, but if he was able to get the photos, he'd pay Paula fifty dollars more than what they'd agreed on.

"If I can be in Santa Fe half a day. . ."

Taking one photo after another, continuously reloading one of the three cameras he carried—all of them small, automatic, covered with black electrical tape so they wouldn't be too conspicuous (he used a technique that he himself had perfected in order to take photos from waist-level, or holding the camera in his hand but without lifting it to his face, imitating the gun-slingers of the Wild West, the New Yorker's heroes in his childhood and now his teachers) although with his unmistakable look of a gringo and his formidable size it was hard for him

94

to pass unnoticed—was his way of showing Paula how happy he was, or how much he liked a place; the moment he stopped reaching his big hand into his knapsack to take out another roll of film, she immediately took him to another spot. His ability to get bored was amazing.

"And what's with that dude . . . ?" some of them asked, after the New Yorker passed by.

They stopped in front of a dismembered doll. It wasn't the only one. Most of them were made of plastic and were hollow. There was something of everything: legs, arms, heads, torsos . . . some seemed to come to life, but it wasn't so, it was the children dedicated to reducing the size of the piles and, according to their size, carrying arms, legs, and heads similar to those they'd lost a little while ago. The children, nevertheless, kept growing. The dump was also growing. The line of trucks reached back until it lost itself in the distance among the hills of cans, glass, paper, metal . . . Everything is the color of mud, Paula thought, the bulldozer that competes with dogs, cows that graze placidly among the cans, children and men who separate the refuse.

The New Yorker went from one side to the other, exclaiming out loud about the beauty, the surrealism, the art, the wonder of that place. When they'd gone to the police station to get the permit, Lem had said, addressing the official to convince him of his good faith and that his motives were purely aesthetic, that he loved the work of Toledo and Leonora Carrington. He was a great admirer of Mexican art.

"A *coffee-table book*," Lem said, with the permit now in his hand.

Paula commented that the idea seemed strange to her and that she couldn't imagine a book of photos on the Santa Fe garbage dump in the living room of her home and, even less, next to

Dalí or *Mexican Flowers*, for example. Lem insisted that it would be a success in the United States, above all in the richest, most liberal neighborhoods of the biggest cities like Los Angeles or New York.

"On the back cover someone can write about the human condition or Christ's beatitudes from the Sermon of the Mount."

She'd seen other photos from this new stage of Lem's, they were fragmentary, with bold primary colors, without any apparent aesthetic pretension or planning, which gave them a somewhat unreal and naïve atmosphere. It was a very New York project, was Paula's only response, and it might be successful.

They were allowed to wander through the dump under the condition that they not take photos. Which Lem ignored, of course. Paula climbed onto a plateau of dry, compact earth that was used as a soccer field. It was windy there and the smell, sweet and nauseating, was even stronger than below. Still, it seemed less disagreeable because she could distract herself watching a group of girls playing, then three dogs, and finally a boy with a man who, by the way he treated him, seemed to be his father. It was the only spot that barely resembled a plaza or a public garden.

It overlooked all of Santa Fe and, at the other end of the valley, the volcanoes. It was one of those dusks of a paralyzing transparency, the surrounding hills dark and silent, the colors dense and clean, blue for the most part, tending towards darkness, night, to what was aqueous and deep. But the humidity, almost palpable if one extended a hand, was denied by the clarity, the weightlessness of the air and light. She looked toward the sky and after a silence that she felt she was losing herself in, she heard a voice.

"Let's go." It was Lem. "This light makes it impossible to do anything."

She felt tired, bothered by that smell that would stay with her for weeks. She tried to walk through the less muddy parts and it annoyed her that Lem did it so carelessly. He seemed to enjoy sticking his big boots in the mud and water, and he didn't do anything to clean them before getting into the car.

"You don't look very happy," the New Yorker observed.

"And what happened?" Ana wanted to know, when they stopped laughing. "Did he keep insisting?"

Their "happy hour" conversation hadn't changed, but it had been reduced to a request that Paula go to bed with him. He wasn't romantic, neither did he tell her that he loved her, nor pretend that their relationship could transcend or endure. He told her about his adventures with other women and reminded her that on his travels he'd slept with mulatto, oriental, black, Slavic, Latina, Danish women . . .

"There was no need for you to leave New York," Paula said.

It didn't make Lem laugh. He took his sexual anthropology very seriously. When he began to say what he'd do with her, Paula excused herself. It entertained her to listen to his stories but they seemed more comical than sensual, although she never told him that. Sometimes she imagined what it would be like to get naked with Lem and what was strongest was always the smell. A blend of mud, clay, and garbage from Santa Fe, then body odors that varied in intensity according to whether Lem had bathed one, two, or three days earlier; the smell of marijuana or hashish, since Lem said that he never fucked without smoking beforehand; but, most of all, finally, the chemical smell, on his fingertips, of developing fluid and the plastic of the film.

"In spite of already spending some time out of the Big Apple," Ana added, "he'd also smell like *bagels*, cream cheese, sour pickles, peanut butter, soy sauce, yogurt, *Kentucky Fried Chicken*, apple pie, *McDonald's* hamburgers . . . My God, it would make anyone hungry!"

They laughed and Paula told Ana that it was impossible to talk seriously to her.

They ordered dessert, cappuccinos, and drank what was left of the bottle of red wine.

"So, though you might not believe it, I went to look for him."

"I believe I might have done the same thing," Ana said, reflectively. "But did you really like him?"

"Truthfully, no. He kept insisting. He became very boring on the phone, sometimes drunk or high, and he always ended by pleading that he needed me, he desired me, complaining about his own depressive and melancholy state, and then he added the address of the hotel and his room number in case I decided to visit him! As if I didn't know how to get there." It wasn't very late. In the hotel they knew her although she'd never entered further than the lobby and the restaurant-bar. One of the receptionists greeted her and offered to ring the room for her. She assented with a nod, looking for Lem with her gaze. No one answered in Room 411 and Paula said it wasn't important and that she preferred to leave him a note under his door. She crossed the half-empty space cast in the shadow of the restaurant-bar without seeing him. She walked slowly although she was getting more nervous. When she got to the bathroom, she let the cold water run over her wrists and then slid a wet paper towel over her neck. She combed her hair and redid her makeup, thinking all the time that it was better not to look for the photographer but, at the same time, sure that she was going up to the fourth floor.

That afternoon she'd gone to the garbage dump. The guard at

the entrance, who now knew Paula and greeted her smiling just like some of the collection-truck drivers did, told her that he hadn't seen Lem. She stayed in her car, curled up in the back seat, on a quiet street on the upper part of Reforma. She was used to that refuge, since her university days, when she sometimes did the same thing between classes. Today she felt the need to be alone for a while, in an unknown place, as if she were a stranger and it didn't matter to her what others thought if they happened to see her. The garbage dump depressed her, and even more so the pile of dolls where she'd gone to look for Lem. Without completely losing awareness of being in the back of a Caribe with her face turned toward the seat, her face pressed to the fabric so that her own breath comforted her, eyes closed but perceiving as if from a distance the light from the streetlamp and the tall trees, she slept a while. When she woke it was already night. She'd dreamt something sad and blurry about her childhood and the house in Brazil. When she sat down, she decided to look for Lem in his hotel.

There was no movement in the corridors and she had to wait until a *bellboy* appeared. She pretended to have forgotten her key. She gave him a tip before going alone into the room and locking the door behind her. The maid had left everything in its place and the lamps on the bureau were turned on. There was clothing from the laundry-service on the bed. It seemed as if no one had slept in the room recently and, nevertheless, all of Lem's belongings, or most of them, were there, slightly in disarray, on the dressing-table and in the open suitcase.

Paula told herself she didn't have the right to be there. What did it matter if Lem spent his nights outside; the hotel staff would understand perfectly, maybe it was common with certain guests. She remembered the first time they'd worked together. Lem had been one of the first foreign reporters to arrive in Mexico City after the earthquake. Because of her knowledge of English and the city, Paula had worked with him as a guide and interpreter, forty-eight hours in which they almost hadn't slept and which seemed like a week because of all the places and the strong impressions, one after another. The stadiums and the government offices, improvised like morgues, the desks like slabs, the countless covered-up bodies, and the smell that seemed like death, although she didn't know the smell of death, all of it, for her was a silent movie: the soundtrack—the shouts, the weeping, the interviews—had been erased, but not the images and the smell. Some time after Lem had returned to New York, Paula received the front page and some important inside pages of the *New York Times* with her name, together with Lem's, at the bottom of the photos. The relationship had been intense, professional, personal in spite of their not saying anything about themselves, and Paula had remained with a pleasant impression of Lem, she felt affection maybe because of what they'd seen together or because of the New Yorker's capacity to be moved. She also admired him. She didn't hear any news of him until he returned a year later and looked for her.

Before leaving, she wanted to stick her head into the bathroom. She went halfway in, touching the wall with her hand until she found the light switch. She saw herself reflected in the mirror but she also noticed something in the top-right corner. It was a strip of negatives—she had to rest her hands and a knee on the sink to really see it—of the children in front of the piles of dismembered dolls. She felt disturbed. What had she gone to look for there? Did she want Lem to make love to her? She didn't like him physically, he even seemed a little repulsive to her. Had she really wanted to find the photographer? And, if not, what was she doing in his room?

Given everything and Paula's silence, Ana didn't insist that she continue talking. After taking a few sips of her cappuccino and both lighting another cigarette, Paula continued.

The next time they saw each other, she didn't remark that she'd gone to look for him, although she did tell him that she couldn't accompany him as often as before. In reality, she wanted to stop seeing him, but not tell him that all of a sudden. She was thinking of gradually spacing out their afternoons together. Now, the times she gave him a ride to the garbage dump, she left him at the entrance and then went to *Vips* in Cuajimalpa to read and study. She returned for him and on the way back to the hotel they didn't say anything. He'd changed a lot; he paid even less attention to how he dressed, and his scruffiness was also a little obsessive as far as his behavior and his way of speaking. They hadn't abandoned the ritual of going to the hotel bar to have a drink before saying goodbye, but now Lem didn't go to his room to get cleaned up and change clothes, he entered the restaurant just as he'd arrived from the garbage dump and the waiter directed them to a table next to the kitchen on one side, and an air-duct on the other. He stayed until late at night. He drank a lot and ate almost anything for dinner: French fries, *quesadillas* or a pizza. Paula used to leave after a while, the time it took her to finish her drink.

She noticed he was anxious and when she commented on that to him, Lem said it must be because of his divorce, which was in process, and to have to report on natural disasters, poverty, hunger, corruption . . . in order to send money to his ex-wife and take charge of the *ivy-league* education of his offspring. Which was true; in '85 he'd already commented to Paula that he wasn't living with his family in Queens, but in a hotel. He added that there was something else and asked Paula to accompany him the next day to the garbage dump.

"Do you see it?" he asked, now in front of the pile of dolls and surrounded by children who played with him and saw him as a kind of buffoon. Lem was used to that treatment: in many parts of the world, being surrounded by children had been his passport and safe-conduct. Besides, the affection he showed them was sincere. With his long beard, more like an adolescent's than an apostle's, and the clash between his way of dressing and behaving and his age of fifty-something, it was easy to make him the brunt of jokes and fun. He had the grace and lightness of corpulent people—she would have to see him dance, Paula thought—which gave him an amiable air, recently darkened now that he almost never laughed.

"No, what?" Paula asked.

"They don't recognize you," said Lem.

She hadn't thought of that. But it was true, some of them should have recognized her. She'd gone there often and recently. "It's because of apathy or malnutrition," she said, in English. "Or maybe it's because of the turpentine or glue they sniff."

"And you, do you recognize any of them?"

Paula looked at them. "No."

"The children are never the same," said Lem.

"They work in shifts," Paula said.

"No, I don't think so."

He was silent for a while and then, walking away with Paula toward the soccer field, said: "I imagine the children becoming dolls. It began as a game and now I can't free myself of that idea. Look, the spaces between the frames could represent fractions of a second or whole minutes. There's no way of knowing at what speed it's happening. I haven't been able to discover it. I know that it's a fantastic idea, but even so, it disturbs me."

Paula noted that Lem's eyes were brimming with tears. She felt tenderness for him and embraced him.

"Don't pay attention to me. It's that I miss my children."

"You should let this go," Paula told him. "It's not doing you any good."

He didn't show her the photos now—those from the garbage dump as well as of people in other parts of the city—and because of what she'd seen that day, Paula supposed that he wasn't using the cameras now although he continued carrying them. She'd protested that it seemed aggressive to photograph people like that, and he answered that the aggression was necessary and indispensable. A photographer robbed images. He had to impose himself, inspire shock and respect, although it might only be to flee afterwards like a coward or disappear. She didn't know what he was living on, or when his funds would run out, or if he was thinking about returning to New York. He hadn't reported to the newspaper office. At the beginning, he'd made references to United Nations sponsorship for a project on cities with major problems scheduled for the year 2000, but now he only smiled when Paula asked him about it. It had been weeks since he'd spoken about art or sociology, or modernism and post-modernism, in relation to the garbage dump.

"The truth is that photography interests me less and less," Paula heard. "I don't know if I've told you, but I'm the great-grandson of a Russian rabbi who emigrated and ended up in New York. Doesn't it seem absurd to you? The only religious part of my upbringing was my paternal grandfather who was convinced that I'd have my *bar mitzvah*. My parents are agnostics. A sister of my mother converted to Catholicism and my father said that she was the third Jew in his building to do the same thing because it was fashionable in certain New York Jewish communities to be Catholic. Lately I've been thinking a lot about that. 'Who wouldn't return voluntarily as a slave to Egypt?' my mother said whenever something went badly. On another occasion—I must have been eight years old—she got on her knees beside me and very seriously, almost solemnly, expressed to me what I later understood was her credo: '. . . you belong to a dispossessed people that wanders in search of its country of origin, and everywhere you see the beauty of God but it's no longer for you.' Maybe she heard it from her grandfather. My mother wasn't a Zionist, she was a very pragmatic millionaire and her homeland was New York. I lost all the money my parents had willed to me before I reached forty. I believe that I've been in every big city in the world. I've never had my own house, I've paid rent or lived in hotels. A month after beginning divorce proceedings, my wife informed me that she was going to buy the house where we'd lived and paid rent for fifteen years. She does the right thing. You know, Paula, I feel guilty. I feel very guilty."

That day, Lem explained that he wanted to go up to his room right away.

"Will you be alright?" Paula asked him.

"Yeah, don't worry."

"Order your dinner brought up."

"Yeah, I'll do that."

He didn't ask her to stay, doing that would have put Paula in a distressing situation now that she felt more affection than ever but also the certainty that, for her, what was attractive about Lem wasn't something physical. For a moment Lem had seemed old to her.

Later that night Paula called the hotel and he answered and said that he'd smoked a joint and, praise God, it relaxed him, like always. He'd had rougher times and now he intended to sleep.

"And did you have some dinner?"

"Sure did! Pot always gives me an appetite."

Paula laughed.

"You don't know what I'd give if you were here by my side . . . I'm going to have to return to New York."

"Why?"

"Even the garbage dump looked beautiful today."

"You really are seriously ill."

"I wish that were the only thing. I think I've fallen in love."

"Don't lose sleep, Lem. Good night."

She didn't hear anything about him that week, but at the end of it, he began looking for her again. They agreed on seeing each other in the restaurant-bar of the hotel. When Paula arrived, Lem had been drinking for a while although he swore that it was his first drink. He was very excited and the topic of his conversation was entropy. He was saying that it was impossible to be a photographer and not feel fascinated by the contemplation of change. It was a fascination ultimately morbid, because change—at least the most obvious kind—was the same as decay, dispersion, disorder. Energy didn't disappear, it dispersed, and took mysterious shapes, that is, ones that were invisible and, practically speaking, non-existent. What better example than Mexico City! Paula had seen more changes than a New Yorker, Parisian, or Londoner four times her age. Paula was an old woman at twenty-something years of age. And to believe that change was equal to improvement was a crass mistake. Lem wanted permanence so much and, nevertheless, everything was speeding up, becoming the same, losing itself:

the Mexico City of Paula's great-grandparents, of her grandparents or parents, of her own childhood . . . including the houses they'd lived in.

"Bombings weren't necessary here."

"You're a nostalgic man," Paula said.

"Well, if you don't believe me it's because you've never been married," he said and Paula thought that he used that phrase often.

Lem was silent long enough to order two more *Old Fashioned*'s. It was no longer "happy hour" but he told the waiter that it seemed like a good way to serve drinks any time. Paula ordered an individual pizza and a Coke. She didn't speak; that's how it was in general between them: he liked to tell his stories and she liked listening to him.

"This matter of entropy," Lem continued, "reminds me of Sloane in *As I Lay Dying*. He was a lazy man because it cost him effort to begin anything but, also, to stop himself once he started. The buzzards were flying over him as they normally do, in circles and over what's already dead. They're wise creatures that understand this energy principle. Although they go too far at times, like certain African vultures I got to photograph: after eating so much rotting flesh, they leapt instead of flying! Their beaks, red and bulging . . . "

"Like an alcoholic's," Paula interrupted him and regretted it.

"What I couldn't tell you about Africa," Lem continued, pretending that he hadn't heard her.

When Paula's pizza arrived, Lem observed her without saying anything. He drank two more *Old Fashioned*'s before pronouncing what he'd do with her. Paula knew this wasn't like other times and that she should leave as soon as possible, although she was afraid of leaving him alone. Lem insisted on accompanying her to the car and once there wanted to press her against the door to force a kiss on her.

"I don't want to!" she shouted and pushed him away.

In the morning, Paula left a letter for him with the receptionist, telling him it would be best if they no longer saw each other. For his part, the New Yorker left an envelope for Paula at the newspaper office and when she went to pick it up saw that it only contained the exact amount of money Lem still owed her. Her father advised the newspaper that Paula would be out for a week.

Lem kept insisting. Paula's father answered on one occasion and told her that Lem had called the house and asked her to please not see him. It was the tone of voice, soft but forceful, that her father used when he was giving an order.

"What did he want?" Paula asked.

"I don't know, but he seemed a little beside himself. Agitated. He insisted on speaking to me in Spanish."

"How was he 'beside himself'?"

"I don't know, very tense, he wanted to speak as quickly in Spanish as he does in English. According to him, I understood him perfectly. I told him, in English, to be sure, that I'd give you his message and that you'd speak to him if you wanted to. I also told him not to call the house any more."

"And you haven't seen him again?" Ana asked.

"No," Paula said. "It worries me. At the newspaper, they haven't heard anything about him. I think he returned to New York. He hasn't called the house for three or four days, either. *No news is good news*, I suppose."

They talked about other things. As they left the restaurant, she said goodbye to Ana with the intention of returning home, but once in the car, and around the San Antonio intersection, instead of taking Revolución going south, she took Patriotismo toward downtown. She decided to look for him. She thought that there must have been some reason they'd talked so much about Lem.

In the hotel, she went up to the fourth floor without stopping and walked directly to his room. It was strange to find the door unlocked when she turned the knob. She pushed lightly, not before counting to ten. The furniture was all against the walls and in the middle of the room there was a kind of pyramid made of all the dolls' limbs. He'd brought them from Santa Fe, one by one, or a few at a time. Around the pyramid he'd placed lamps, screens, shades, tripods, and cameras, in such a way that it looked a lot like a studio. The room, nevertheless, smelled bad, of sweat, alongside the acrid smell of burnt cables. The equipment was turned off but the heat led her to believe that Lem hadn't left the room until just now, to buy cigarettes or some food and because of that had left the door unlocked. She looked again at the pile and remembered something and at the same time knew that that something was what had been hovering around her these last weeks.

She was pinned against the wall. They were looking for the "Midnight Man." Her father carried her on his shoulders and when he thought it was safe they would plunge back into the passing crowd, only to be flung and pushed from one place to another until they arrived—Paula didn't know how—on the other side of the narrow street. Her father left her seated on a window-sill where she was supposed to wait for him and not move for any reason. She saw him disappear in the procession to look for his wife who had remained in some bar, accompanied by Esteban, the family driver.

They succeeded in meeting up. Her mother said that as long as her husband was with Paula, it didn't matter that they were separated. She was very tired, dazed by the crowd, she wanted to return to the hotel, but had discovered that there weren't any taxis or buses returning to Recife. The crowd was in an uproar: they fought for the privilege of standing near the *Hombre*, next to and in front of the band and, because of that, they stamped their feet, they shook their arms, they shouted. The bursts of aggression were like sparks or small explosions, Paula thought, points of contact more than fights. The crowd seemed to open and close around her, people interlaced to form chains or what looked like a big sea-serpent. It was exciting but she didn't let go of her father's hand. He asked her often if she was having fun. She looked so out of place, dancing *forró* clumsily but with great enthusiasm. She assured him that she was. Her mother had also made an effort, but now, tired out, sat down at a table in the plaza where they'd been at the start of the evening.

A young woman approached. She leaned against Sr. Neira, joking and pinching his cheek. She ignored Sra. Neira and Paula. She called Sr. Neira a thief and insisted that she wanted pot. She told him that his daughter in São Paulo was already eight years old.

"But I was only there six months ago for the first time," Sr. Neira said, also joking.

"Thief!" she said and cackled. "But you've visited me on so many occasions, eh? It doesn't matter when it was. The moment of conception only matters for the Virgin. Your daughter is very pretty. This one, too," she added, looking for the first time at Paula, out of the corner of her eye.

"How nice. She must look like her mother."

The woman, feeling flattered, winked. "Well, yeah, a bit."

Sra. Neira didn't move. Paula didn't understand much of the conversation between the woman and her father but she saw that both were having fun. She suggested to him, very unsubtly, that they meet later. She was pretty, Paula thought, but she looked tired and her face was swollen.

"To remember old times," she told him.

"OK, where?" Sr. Neira asked.

"Thief!" she repeated and pinched his cheek again. "You know very well where! but that's in São Paulo, right? Here I'm in the Félix Hotel. She kissed her fingertips and then touched him on the cheek a few times, then she leaned toward him and lightly kissed the tip of his nose. She moved away, swaying her hips and looking back over her shoulder. Paula noticed that the fabric covering her revealed the outline of her panties. Her father observed her moving away and then took a few sips of his beer.

Her mother didn't say anything or move. Her gaze was fixed on a point of the table.

"You shouldn't let it bother you," her father said. "It's obvious she was looking for marijuana or money, and also to annoy or offend us. But that didn't happen. Besides, she seemed nice."

"Charming. And don't flatter yourself: it's difficult to imagine myself offended or bothered by a whore."

Sr. Neira glanced at his watch. Only a few hours were left before the night ended. A man in the plaza was preaching about the All Powerful One, the love of Christ and his presence. On their way to the highway, Esteban recounted and explained that the *Midnight Man* had died from cardiac arrest inside the giant papier mache figure at the head of the procession. He'd played the role for many years.

Sra. Neira not only went to her daughter's room but moved all her belongings, clothes, toiletries, shoes, bags. She reclosed the door that connected Paula's room with the adjoining living room in the suite. She was in the bathroom a long time and Paula imagined her crying. She was worried and didn't know if she should look for her. She'd never felt very close to her mother and preferred to stay in bed waiting for her. When she finally came out of the bathroom, she got into the other bed without turning on the light so she wouldn't wake her daughter. Paula watched her back; she seemed to be still crying. She felt very bad, tense, trapped, without being able to decide whether to speak to her or get in the other bed and hold her. She felt that it was her fault. She'd insisted they go to Carnival, in spite of the fact that Sebastián had accepted an invitation to be part of Sr. Rosellini's crew to sail an enormous white sailboat along the coast of Brazil, setting sail from Rio and traveling toward the south, and that her mother's usual reaction was of near-disgust regarding any expression of popular culture.

Her father had wanted to accompany Sebastián, and although the invitation also included him, rowing in the small man-made lake of Chapultepec Park made him very sick, irremediably so, no matter what medication the family doctor prescribed for him. Sr. Rosellini told him that he wasn't thinking of losing sight of the coast, but to Paula's father the trip suggested an intense, prolonged torture, and having a constant view of the land promised to aggravate, more than diminish, a bad situation. He told Sebastián that if his mother and sister insisted on going to Carnival, he'd have to accompany them. Paula knew that a birthday wish would be granted almost magically. Up until now, he'd never refused a reasonable request.

She couldn't sleep, nor did she want to. She feared having to see her parents the following morning. She didn't hear the door from the other bedroom open or close. She waited until her mother was sleeping, she dressed herself in the same clothes, and left the room, as well as the hotel, without being seen. She had the money they'd given her for her birthday.

What served her as a guide was a photo of her *nana* Solange, with some family members, in front of the *Nosso Senhor do Bonfim* church. She arrived by bus, a trip lasting many hours, and walked to the church. She liked the blueness and intimate size of the chapel's interior. The ceiling and walls were crowded with heads, arms, legs, different limbs made out of wood, plaster, metal, ceramic, plastic, the colors varied and not always dark. There were notes and photos, drawings stuck to the limbs or directly onto the wall. Paula approached. A girl, her age, asked God to help her pass her high school exam. Another note gave thanks for a woman's recuperation from Leukemia: a drawing done with crayons showed her lying in bed. On another sheet of paper she read: "When will you come, Lord, to spill your blood on this dry earth?" She looked at the ceiling again. There were dolls very similar to some that she had in her room. She had a sensation of uneasiness.

She asked herself which limbs had belonged to the same body. She tried to put them back together like in the game *memoria*, but instead of turning the cards face-up and trying to match them, she glanced back and forth trying to choose parts to reshape a single body, or several complete bodies. She entertained herself, then got bored and ended up feeling very lonely, as if she wanted to cry. She'd never believed she could find Solange.

Now, entering the bathroom, she saw that the plastic curtain was drawn. She felt that behind the amber green there was a body; she drew back the plastic and when she saw Lem, seated in the tub, she kept pulling the curtain and swallowing a scream, although the other was rocking without looking at her, his eyes closed, senselessly moving back and forth. It's the prostrated state of my mother, Paula thought, although she barely saw that now. Lem was groaning or singing very softly, with part of his head and shoulders wrapped in a towel he held with his hands, and Paula again thought of Solange although the groans of her *nana* had been different, sometimes she'd laugh like a girl, her joy infecting Paula, not like what Lem was doing, which seemed opaque, monotonous, and sad to her, but when she looked at him again she knew that he wasn't so different, what the New Yorker was doing was praying, and, even more so, the same way that Solange did those nights she'd entered her bedroom to recite the rosary, Lem's prayers included her. Paula lifted her face. Her own weeping seemed to descend from the top of her head and rise from her throat, filling her mouth.

The Taste of Salt

*to Sergio Mondragón, dear friend and kind reader
from the beginning*

*The almost insoluble task is to let neither the power of
others, nor our own powerlessness stupefy us.*
—THEODOR ADORNO,
MINIMA MORALIA

*So truth is, in time, the absurd and fertile quest of lies,
which we pay with tears and blood.*
—EDMOND JABÈS

Maybe I have to write something before trying to open a file. Being a klutz as far as computers go and so stubborn in my clumsiness, as only a reluctant sexagenarian can be, including about changing the place where he's eaten every day for years, in spite of the fact that the food is no longer what it was, is only one of the many ways I'm described by my daughter, who's kind and well-meaning, but since she's become a mother, she's that for everyone, including her progenitor. And she's been a mother for many years, with numerous offspring, maybe in response to being an only daughter. I'd eat at her house, but I eat better—given everything and the change in ownership—in the place where she used to go with me on certain occasions, before she got married. I'd never tell her that, of course. I won't throw that in her face; she's never liked the kitchen. I spend my time with them on Sundays, when my son-in-law wisely orders take-out or invites all of us to the Danubio or the Bellinghausen. María Fernanda has offered to give me some lessons on the computer but I've told her I prefer to enter my battles alone. And unarmed, she adds. I'm thinking of using this device—a gift from one of my grandchildren; he studies computer-programming and, when he changed models, he gave me the old one as a gift—almost the way I'd use an electric typewriter. A word processor, Enrique told me. I looked at him, annoyed. That's what it's called, he explained. Oh, I understand, I said, I thought you were referring to me.

It's not this that I want to write about, but the death of my friend. The business about the computer is relevant because I'm seated in front of one, because Joaquín Ballesteros Landero learned to use one since they appeared in his work with the government and, before that, as a journalist, and because in some way I relate that glowing screen, which he sat in front of for hours—what am I saying, years!—to cryptography and his death. If he'd entrusted everything to the computer, maybe they wouldn't have killed him.

I myself don't know which has caused me more pain, Ballesteros's death or his wife's grief. I know Lourdes very well. We've been colleagues for many years in the School of Philosophy and Letters at UNAM. Although both of us are historians, her time has been more dedicated to research, mine to teaching,

116

which makes us similar as far as vocation but different as far as practice. I believe that I was the first person whom she told. Why? Several possibilities occur to me. I'm also a widower and she helped me a lot when I lost my wife. Our friendship began long before Elena's death; it was a friendship for four voices, in which there was a tacit understanding that it wasn't necessary for us to give undeserved importance to our weaknesses, just as we'd never tolerate lies. I believe that there was an aspect of our relationship that was clear for all four of us that made it, it seems to me, even richer and long-lasting. Elena knew that if I had to choose between Joaquín and Lourdes as friends, I'd choose Lourdes. Elena would choose Joaquín. Joaquín, Elena. And Lourdes, me. We never spoke about it. It wasn't necessary. What remains clear—that phrase is laughable—: if I had to choose between Lourdes and Elena, I always would have chosen Elena. I believe I can say that Lourdes would always have chosen Joaquín, since that's what she's always done. I'm not sure about Joaquín or Elena, which is something else that connects me and Lourdes, and maybe the reason why I was the first one to find out that night.

Although Joaquín had stopped seeing most of his friends, and almost never went out, they continued inviting me to their house, above all at dinner-time, or in the afternoon, when we shared tea and biscuits, a custom of Joaquín's that came from two sources: his mother was Chilean with English parents, and Joaquín had done his post-graduate studies in England. But many times he didn't join us, and not because he wasn't at home, but because he'd locked himself up in his studio, which he'd ordered built on the roof and which could be reached either from inside the house—a staircase in the hall on the second floor—or from the spiral staircase on the patio. Although opening the space on the

roof had been a project that wasn't cheap and, yes, was inconvenient, one that filled the whole house with noise and dust for
more time than the five days the head brick-layer had promised,
now only Joaquín used the spiral staircase, as if it were the only
one that existed. At night, Lourdes climbed the inside stairs
to knock on the door and let him know dinner was ready. He
responded and even so went down by the outside stairs to enter
the kitchen. Lourdes recognized that the construction of the
second means of access had been at her insistence, and that from
the beginning Joaquín had said it wasn't necessary and wasn't
thinking of using it.

When time permitted and we had our tea on the patio, sometimes Joaquín appeared at the window to greet me. Lourdes
always wanted to bring him up a tray, but he'd insisted, sharply,
for her not to since it could be dangerous. At first he invited her
into the studio, following her up the back stairs but after a few
months, he stopped doing it. I only knew his studio from what
Lourdes told me about it. He'd taken everything with him except
the piano, since they might have had to remove the windows in
the living room to take it out to the patio and, from there, lift it
to roof-level with ropes and pulleys to set it in the studio before
completing the construction. Its transfer created too many problems. He comes downstairs to visit the piano and his wife, in
that order, joked Lourdes.

They no longer had a maid. If that hadn't been so, Lourdes
would have sent her up with the tray. In fact, the maid's room
was the humble origin of her husband's studio. He didn't want
full-time servants. None of their children lived with them, and
Lourdes assured me that the lack of servants was by common
agreement, a matter of privacy and lifestyle, not of money. A
woman came two times a week to help her with the heaviest

118

chores. "My husband shut up in the servant's room, and me seated on the patio, sipping the tea he likes so much, hoping he'll reappear." She laughed as she said this and invented different ways of describing the situation, which seemed ironic and amusing to her.

The only one who went up to visit him, when Joaquín left the door open, was the German Shepherd. He'd learned on his own to climb that metal spiral, with his body almost touching the steps, as if he were thinking of sliding on his belly more than advancing on his paws. He didn't look down. Joaquín often opened the window and shouted at him to climb the metal stairs. When the door—visible from the patio—was closed, the German Shepherd remained lying under the shade of the fig tree. He has the wisdom of mountain-climbers, Lourdes said, and their common sense. He fears heights and senses that it's much harder to go down than up. He also liked—in fact, Lourdes was sure that he preferred, like she did—the access from inside so he could later lay down in front of the door. Although he was Joaquín's intimate companion, and continues being that of Lourdes at this writing, I don't remember his name. I don't remember that they called him by his name very much although they must have. I'll stop talking this way about the animal because he was the only one who witnessed what happened that night. He was also the one who made it clear to Lourdes that Ballesteros had died.

What to do when one has lost a document that's supposedly on file but that doesn't appear? I could call my nephew—he was the one who gave me the gift of this marvelous instrument that would save me so much time and effort—but I'm afraid that I've bothered him enough with this and other similar questions. Without a printer, losing files this way is the essence of ephemeral art. Of ephemeral writing, then. Of writing that vanishes with the light of the screen. That could be an ideal situation, if it weren't that there are those who know how to recover and discover what one believed was lost. When there are letters left over, because of mistakes I've made, instead of deleting them, I leave them on the screen. They'll be useful to me later, like signs that fall into place, even if it's the second round. They accumulate, nevertheless, with alarming speed, like a limb that doesn't stop growing. If sins entered the world because of only one mistake, what I write would probably fill several worlds.

Joaquín kept the diskettes in perfect order in a special box. It was the only thing, except for his person and his clothes, that traveled from the studio to the bedroom when he finished working, and returned with him to the studio in the morning. That day, whoever entered the studio had taken the box and who knows how many other documents. Lourdes knew that the explanation of the incident as a house-robbery wasn't the truth, or that it was but hadn't happened the way the press understood it, since the thieves, instead of taking whatever object of material or sentimental value, had destroyed everything. It wasn't the anger and frustration of someone who doesn't find anything very valuable but, rather, the impassioned pleasure of someone who destroys what he hates, or the frustration and impotence of someone who doesn't find what he's looking for. The other explanations that the PGR offered, or that appeared in society as if they were true, not only didn't interest Lourdes but visibly sickened her when she even heard them coming out of someone's mouth.

The secretary of state, the national attorney general, and the governor of ___ went personally, and separately, to her house to express their condolences and to offer their unconditional support and their help with whatever might be necessary. After praising the life and work of her husband, without lowering the

120

coffee cup he was holding, the governor asked Lourdes, in a cordial manner but lowering his voice as if others might be present and could hear them, if her husband had entrusted her with any document or piece of writing. It would be a great help in getting to the bottom of the case.

"Do you believe that our personal correspondence would interest someone?" Lourdes asked him.

The governor became embarrassed.

"No, I wasn't referring to that type of documentation."

"In that case, no," responded Lourdes. "Would you like some more coffee?"

"Thank you very much." The governor shook his head to indicate no.

Her husband was a very intelligent man, continued the governor, but his delusion was wanting to see everything—or his belief that he could. That conversation with the governor, with whom her husband had worked closely during his campaign and at the beginning of his term, shook up Lourdes the same way, although without the same force, as when she'd discovered Joaquín dead. Lourdes assured the governor that her husband had deliberately crammed everything into the study, since when he decided to work at home, he'd promised Lourdes he would keep those two worlds separate so that the change wouldn't involve his taking over the house. It was Lourdes who insisted that it wasn't necessary, that she preferred to have him closer, that it seemed like a good idea for him to retire—she viewed it as an indefinite sabbatical—to write his memoirs, but that it wasn't necessary to exile himself to the roof of the house. She didn't tell the last part to the governor but to me.

She'd resisted the idea that Joaquín had taken his life; still, she couldn't shake off her doubts. Her husband's behavior was very far from being typical. Before his death they'd spent three years that had seemed three times that; his obsession of remembering everything, but even more than that, of including it all in his memoirs—as if life could be poured into a text—had significantly aged him. His friends had stopped visiting him. And who could blame them! For Joaquín, while he was in his studio, any visit was inconvenient, and since he spent more and more time in his studio, it was very embarrassing for them to arrive at the house without stepping into the living-room, so that Lourdes might go for Joaquín, only to return with the news that he was indisposed. Now, every once in a while, they'd call and speak to Lourdes to see how both were doing.

At the beginning, Lourdes would go out, making an attempt to continue with life as normal, visiting her friends at their homes or inviting them out to eat. She tried to arrange gatherings with a few friends so her husband could get some rest from work. She organized outings to the outskirts of the city, to Ixtapan de la Sal or to San Juan del Río, or to any other spot since both of them had always loved visiting small towns. The last outing she'd organized was to the Franciscan convents that dot the perimeter of the Popocatepetl volcano, now a world heritage site. He'd accompanied her, but unwillingly and what had excited him so much before now left him indifferent. It was a change that had a strong impact, since her husband had always been a man of many interests, of many passions, who was silent but not self-absorbed, with a handful of close friends and small dinner parties, but not given to solitude. Lourdes began to imitate him, limiting herself to her work like a researcher, reducing her schedule to part-time, and the rest of the time keeping busy with domestic chores, something she'd previously done efficiently but without giving it too much importance. She felt that she should keep Joaquín company, even if it were in such an unusual way and he'd never asked for it, and that her presence helped him work. She hoped that by doing so he'd finish more quickly what he'd set out to do.

He loved to walk for hours, but accompanied by Lourdes or one of their children. Gisela, the youngest, was the only one who entered the studio to talk with him simply because she didn't accept a *no*, even less so from her father. She used to enter through the door inside the house. She wasn't a dog and, besides that, her high-heels got stuck in the cracks. But now she was studying in France and Lourdes didn't have the courage to tell her what had happened. She knew beforehand that Gisela wouldn't forgive her for not telling her so she could be at her father's funeral. But Lourdes didn't see the point, she felt that someone whose life is snatched away can't be considered dead. She feared that Gisela, upon returning from France, wouldn't leave again. Her brothers were married and she'd feel obliged to take care of her mother. She didn't want her to find out from what appeared in the national press. It was absurd to try to keep her far away if, sooner or later, she'd learn about her father's death, but Lourdes pretended, she deceived herself consciously, that France was an isolated place, almost imaginary, where Gisela could continue her youth and her development without inexplicable rifts. In the last months, the only time Joaquín went out was on Sundays to eat at one of their children's homes. He watched the soccer game in silence, or continued the conversation during dessert with a distracted air. Not even his grandchildren could make him smile. The only thing that amused him was playing chess with his older grandchildren, who took turns challenging him; he never conceded anything to them but, even so, he often lost. At home he played the piano.

Still, recently, Lourdes had noticed some hopeful signs. Joaquín began to joke again, or angered her with his usual tricks and then smiled. He came down from the studio when he finished working at night, using the stairs in the house. They'd never stopped making love—thank God!, Lourdes said, if he'd excluded me from his life in that way, I wouldn't have been able to stand it—but also in that respect, Lourdes noted a change for the good. He stayed close to her, the two of them embracing, and sometimes they talked. On one occasion, at dinner, which they ate in the kitchen since Joaquín had come down from the studio, he told her he'd be finishing his memoirs soon. She was very happy but all she did was squeeze his hand. She also noticed another change: the cats and the German Shepherd licked any exposed surface on his body, above all his hands and face.

"Why are they licking you so much?" Lourdes asked him.

"They're looking for salt," he said.

He told her about his visits to his uncle Polo's hacienda when he was a child. His father taught him to offer his palm with the fingers extended and together so the horses would lick it with their long, rough tongues. He especially liked a mare named Jirafa.

That night, she tasted her husband's skin in different places without noticing any great saltiness. But animals perceive much more than we do, Lourdes told me. What couldn't they perceive from the taste of others? Impatiently we pull them away so they won't stop to smell, believing that their interest is distraction, that their attention is a beast's blindness. Imagine that by smelling someone's urine—like dogs do with other dogs in that dialogue across distance—or the traces remaining in a spot where he urinated several days ago, you could know his sex, age, whether you're attracted to him or not ... Perhaps also his

124

size, the color of his eyes, if he's testy or even-tempered . . . They understand molecules better than we do. They already know the stairs we climb, including their DNA. Lourdes often talked like that. Since before what happened. In fact, after Ballesteros was flung out the window, she no longer referred to the special qualities of animals. She grew up on a ranch in Veracruz, and her parents had a number of animals, domestic and exotic, on the property. Her father's projects included a lagoon to breed tilapia and sea-bass, raising nutria, an aviary in the middle of the garden that somehow symbolized the ambivalent relationship the engineer had with other creatures: he wanted exotic things near him. Freeing the birds would mean losing them; caging them in very close quarters would reduce in them what made them fascinating. He was a man who one could say felt pain and anger at the sight of a polluted stretch of river, and who loved to fish. Or who was one of the first naturalists in Mexico, interested in the preservation of species, and also an avid hunter. It would be mean, Lourdes assured me, in case it's occurred to you, to believe that his interest in animals only had to do with a desire to not strip the countryside of his favorite activities. It's undeniable, he was a reactionary, if being a reactionary is a repudiation of change, but he was also conservative, in the best sense of the word. When his favorite jaguar escaped, he gave orders to take him captive but he also sent out word for people to walk armed and gave permission for them to shoot him dead if necessary. It would seem that I'm describing something from the time of Porfirio Díaz but I'm telling you about my own childhood. I know of men, our contemporaries, who, placed in similar circumstances, would grant greater value to their mascots than to the lives of the *campesinos* and their animals. They'd keep quiet about the wild animal roaming freely, dispatch their own people to bring it back alive, and promise the first one who saw it a brand-new pick-up truck. My father was the *patrón*, for sure. I'm not going to pretend he didn't like being one. But I believe that what people felt for him was more affection than fear. I know: you'll tell me that that's how it is, poor people line up and come from far away to kiss the hand of the *patrón* on his saint's day, it's part of the strange idiosyncrasy that governs us. Children would bring him wounded animals they'd found, and the engineer walked as far as the small towns to share his knowledge of raising birds, rabbits, fish and other creatures. My mother preferred cats and dogs.

Important men from different departments of the government were there, some in uniforms, others not. Her oldest son was beside her during the first days. Her other children, as well as a cousin who was a bishop, would keep her company for stretches at a time. Friends she hadn't seen for a long time, from UNAM and the newspaper where Joaquín had worked for so many years, came by the house to pay their respects. The priest of the parish where they went to Mass, and a friend who was a Dominican and whom Joaquín enjoyed talking to, deeply mourned what had happened.

The activity seemed rational, ordered, in that place of destruction and madness, and they were respectful to Lourdes when she didn't let them search the rest of the house, although they returned often to ask her the same thing. She visualized the open piano like a box from which they'd ripped off the paper and torn the cardboard to discover what was inside. They'd do the same as they'd done with the other objects, destroying them to achieve a false homogeneity, forcing them into uniformity, Joaquín's studio as an extension of his body, the intention the same for both, to make them unrecognizable but, at the same time, to take something for keeps. What? They'd acted against their own interests: now it would be much harder to discover what they were looking for among the debris, the remains, the traces. It might have been wiser to leave everything intact and to return on another occasion to begin the search again. But Joaquín's presence, his negative, had made them desperate. Don't lose your heads. Those were the instructions they'd received, but adrenaline, rage, sadistic pleasure, were more powerful than acting "professional."

"It's obvious that this is the work of amateurs," a Lieutenant Senderos had said to her, impeccable and calm, "They're young hoodlums—the press spoke of a street gang—who came to rob and did."

Lourdes thought the opposite: that such destruction could only be explained as the end-result of years of preparation. They'd been methodical, and who better to recognize that than a researcher?

"I don't believe they've robbed anything."

"Only you would know that," the lieutenant responded.

A moment afterward, and alone, Enrique Fuentes, a friend of the family and now also its lawyer, asked Lourdes not to speak with anyone.

How had they been able to enter? If she could answer that question, she'd gain some peace. They hadn't gone upstairs through the inside of the house—since Lourdes used to stay up reading, and her bedroom, which she kept the door open to, led to the hall. She would have heard them. To get to the patio, they would have had to enter through the front door of the house, cross the small foyer, and enter the kitchen in order to go out from there. It was the only way of getting to the patio, aside from leaping over one of the walls that separated it from the neighbors' houses, hard work, not only because it meant crossing over one house to arrive at another, but also because of the height of the walls, which was considerable and raised during the construction of the studio, so that Joaquín could look through the window and have a view of the walls that he himself had painted, and the pyracantha, the plumbago, the bougain-villea, and the three cypresses that needed, argued Ballesteros, additional space to grow. Besides, why hadn't __ (I still don't remember his name) barked? Joaquín didn't lock the doors with a key, which explained in part what happened: they could have sneaked into the studio, surprising him, without his having time to react before they threatened him. It occurred to Lourdes that the next day one of the investigators similarly expressed that the only explanation was that Señor Ballesteros had let in the person or persons (what was most probable, given the destruction and the position of the body, was that there were several men, at least two, who were strong).

The press collected opinions as it does with everything. They followed the questions and the suppositions. Whom had he let enter? Why, if he'd received them so silently and without violence had the visit ended the way it did? Señora Landau de Ballesteros had said, in the investigation, that no one visited them at those hours and that, besides, her husband didn't answer the telephone—he didn't have one in the studio—much less any knock at the door, either during the day or even less so at night, when he revised what he'd written in the morning, almost always listening to music, and ignored the world's existence outside his studio. This open dialogue, the answers, the apparent right of anyone to express his or her opinion, caused an enormous sadness in Lourdes, a rage that could only be expressed through nausea and a feeling of suffocation and feverish heat. Nobody showed interest in stopping the speculations, given everything and the letters directed to the different media and government organizations. The rumors spread horizontally like some cancer that isn't limited to a tissue or organ, and her husband suddenly had links with drug traffickers or had argued with a relative about some matter—inheritance, business, although they hadn't inherited anything recently and weren't owners of any business—or everything was caused by personal revenge, possibly homosexual . . . the latest item in the most scandalous newspapers, which were also the most widely read.

If Joaquín hadn't let them enter, they were already there. She didn't hear anyone else express that opinion. During tense days and insomnia she didn't succeed in shaking off that idea and considering it the only answer. The other idea seemed incredible to her—that they might have burst into the house without her realizing it—although this one seemed incredible too. She reviewed, not only for others, but also for herself, the events of that day. She hadn't left, except in the morning, as she usually did, to go to the historical research center. She returned to prepare lunch, and when she called him, Joaquín came down to the kitchen in order to eat with her. She hadn't received anyone or taken a siesta, she'd passed the afternoon writing a review of a book of Thomas's on the Aztecs, recently published in Mexico and translated into Spanish by a friend of hers, and reading a new chapter of a doctoral dissertation that a student of hers had delivered to her, already some time ago, on the use of theater in the evangelization of New Spain during the Sixteenth Century. She listened to music, but not so loud as to prevent her from realizing what was happening outside the bedroom, which had been her daughter's and that now, since she'd been working at home during the afternoons, Lourdes used as a studio, with minor modifications, emphasizing the impermanence of her presence there and her daughter's stay in Montpellier. In fact, the dressing-table was her desk. She found the seat comfortable, but the mirror disquieting, the part that captured her image was covered with photos, notes, reminders, as if it were a blackboard. Among the different papers, she suddenly saw her eye or the expanse of her skin, irregularly shaped but mostly with straight edges, the color, at a distance, uniform oil-paint broadly applied and in a single stroke, in an almost hurried but sure hand. That collage calmed her. It was a very small space, but as much hers as her husband's studio was his. When she read, she preferred to do so with her feet up, and she reclined in the chaise lounge, whose standing lamp gave good light. She took after her daughter that way. The stereo was also Gisela's. She left the door open, as she was now used to doing with the doors in any room where she found herself.

She didn't deny that the idea they were already there was outlandish. She didn't believe in ghosts, although as a child, at night when she had to leave the big house to walk to the bathroom, on the way there and back, and once inside, lit only by an oil lamp—one that hung above a shelf—she recited all the prayers she'd memorized, asking the intercession of the Virgin, of the saints and of her dead relatives, and feared the devil. At first, her *nana* went with her, but later she insisted on going alone, partly to show that she was now grown up and partly because of the emotion that it stirred up in her. She didn't bump into any specters, and when older, as a teenager, the only ghosts were the characters in history books, or in novels, which she preferred to read at night, when her parents and brothers were asleep. They materialized when she read but more so afterwards, when she turned off the light and remained lying down and quiet in the dark. She closed her eyes and the specters appeared to her, she opened them and they were with her in the half-light of the bedroom. Sometimes she turned on the light again and they were waiting for her in the book she'd placed open and face-down on the bureau. Now the same thing occurred to her when she read letters; she continued the habit of not opening them immediately, so she could keep them and read them at night just before she went to sleep. Much less often, according to who called her, at what hour and from where, she felt something similar when she received a phone call. But that afternoon, and the first hours of the night, she told me that her eyes were open, that she was completely awake.

Ballesteros said that his project would last six weeks. The same amount of time, he stressed, that it took Dostoyevsky to write *The Gambler*. Nevertheless, he built his studio before beginning to write his memoirs. When that didn't make sense to Lourdes, Joaquín's reaction was one of anger. On another occasion, later the same day, he told her it was now time for him to have a studio, and that he wanted to begin working much more at home. He preferred describing his idea to her in English: just as he preferred the word "memoirs" to "autobiography," he preferred "semi-retired" to "retired." The cloistered life that followed had little to do with *semi-retired*. Lourdes made this comment to me, before Ballesteros's death, and when, after I laughed, I asked her if he'd said it, she looked at me obliquely with her head tilted as if I were her student and my question wasn't stupid but definitely impertinent. For me it would be more on target to say that Ballesteros had "walled himself in."

The "memoirs" were a matter of control. Lourdes felt this with growing clarity and certainty. Her first surprise was discovering that Joaquín hadn't begun with what was most recent, his resignation from the governor's team . . . but with his childhood. It's necessary to contextualize what's happened, her husband told her. A phrase that seemed to Lourdes, by turns, pedantic and pretentious. Maybe what happened with the governor . . . was merely the fuse of a mid-life crisis, maybe the crisis was what had detonated the break with the governor, and had its roots in Joaquín's childhood, in his university studies, in his vocation as a journalist and public servant—she insisted on using that description—in his marriage and fatherhood, in his role as a son, a grandson. . . .

The fact was that the gambler, in this case, didn't need six weeks to narrate what he wanted to share, but, up to the present time, a little less than three years. It wasn't clear who was playing with whom or who was playing at what. His memoirs would be a detailed portrait of the collapse of a political system. Lourdes feared that they might also describe the collapse of a life. They made love, tenderly, passionately, with greater intimacy than ever, and in those moments she felt she understood him, although their conversations after sex, when they were still intertwined, included nothing about what he was doing all that time. She knew about his work because Joaquín came down from the studio with a transparent plastic box, inside of which, all arranged, were the diskettes in various colors—a kind of classification—and labeled—another kind, and the only thing that Lourdes could read, without understanding because it was in code.

He told her that now as he approached the end, he was writing what most interested him. It was a denunciation, a *j'accuse*, and he had the necessary facts to back up his accusations. It was the only thing he shared with her and even this seemed too much to him. He said that he shouldn't have told her. That she shouldn't tell anyone. That he didn't want to put her in danger. He asked her to leave the house as little as possible. When, for some reason, she arrived late from the research center, she'd find him seated in the living room or walking in circles in the patio. His spirits had improved, he laughed more and spoke more often about unimportant subjects, but what was on the one hand more relaxed was, on the other, tenser. He now asked her not to bring in food from outside, bought at some restaurant or delicatessen, he asked her if she felt that someone was watching her in the street or had followed her home, although his studio, apart from the big window that looked out onto the patio, also had another that looked out onto the street, but he never appeared at it or opened the curtain. There had been a mistake and he considered sending for the same head brick-layer to cover it up. They'd included it in the design in order to let in daylight and allow the circulation of air.

"I almost never work in the morning," Joaquín told her, on one of those countless occasions in which he'd confided something to her.

"What do you do?"

"I listen to music or I sit in silence."

Smiling, he added:

"Or I look out the window. I follow the lives of the neighbors. The young maids who go up to hang clothes or clean the parakeets' cages. I observe children who sometimes go up there or play in the gardens. There's a young woman who goes out to the balcony to sip her coffee. She does it every morning at the same time and I believe that she knows I observe her. She stirs it with a finger and almost always wears a white robe. It seems to me, although I couldn't swear it, that she's barefoot."

He'd say those things to make her angry. Or to make her laugh, now that the two knew that the only thing that he saw was the ivy, the pyracantha, the bougainvillea or the cypresses growing.

The hard thing was how to establish borders, put limits, choose points of reference. Repression was something inherent in choosing. Lourdes knew it well. Joaquín wanted to include as much as possible, to be in some way exhaustive, as he'd done before, when he was a reporter, although now he himself might be the theme. But to do it, thought Lourdes, he must lock himself up, and then spend hours with his eyes closed. To not read newspapers, or watch television, or want to know anything about the world outside. He would catch up on the news once he finished what he was doing. Interviews had always been his favorite genre.

He'd locked himself in with his own voice or voices. If someone speaks non-stop, writes Maurice Blanchot, he finally becomes closed up. The same thing can be said about someone who writes. When she entered the studio, it never even passed through Lourdes's mind that her husband had caused the destruction. Afterwards, when she discarded the possibility that others had entered the house without her being aware of it or that Joaquín had opened the door and guided his visitors in silence, she considered the possibility that Joaquín had been alone. Accepting this also meant accepting his suicide, which everyone now took as fact. If this were the case, it was a suicide preceded by a struggle. A struggle is a matter of blows, although on this occasion, the others hadn't left marks on his body.

There was something that suggested struggle in that room, an attempt to take something by force, an insistence that others understand it. Maybe he'd lost his sense of direction, taken some wrong steps, a wrong turn, arriving at the window instead of the door. Or suffered a heart attack that made him whirl in pain—like a dervish—until he fell out the window. It was the tyranny of wanting to know himself, of wanting to understand himself.

The studio was like a coffin, empty of a body and also of voices; a press room where those who speak and those who listen take turns, but all inside Joaquín, and the minutes of the press conference are never published, never reach the numerous readers who are waiting for them. Maybe he'd destroyed everything upon realizing that he hadn't discovered what he was seeking after almost three years of closing himself in, and then had flung himself through the window. It was a frightening idea. For Lourdes, imagining that was to think that her husband had suffered some kind of possession. Or equally possible, going about emptying his life into the text hadn't left anything remaining. Lourdes's weeping was filled with rage against unknown enemies.

She didn't trust the official version—given everything and that her relatives accepted it, not directly but through the expression "he who is silent consents," including two of her children. . . which wounded her enormously. Lourdes was interested in the truth of what had happened. "What is the truth?" asked one of her sons, irritated by his mother's insistence. She turned and left.

Her husband was capable of that kind of force, in spite of not being large. When he became angry, he was capable of things that later amazed him. There are numerous anecdotes regarding this, but I'll only name one of them. Joaquín liked mountain-climbing, and had practiced it when he was younger. Now older, above all owing to Lourdes's insistence, he concentrated on another of his favorite pastimes. He went to meetings of a group of friends, the "Rainbow Trout Fishing Club," every first Wednesday of the month at an Italian restaurant in Polanco, near the Parque del Reloj—and I accompanied him on several occasions but I never could understand the attraction of fishing; the gentlemen seemed like youngsters, they spoke with the same kind of enthusiasm as soccer fanatics, but on another level. They ate well, they drank good wine, they exchanged jokes, and small cigars—although some of them, like Joaquín, preferred pipes— they talked about places to fish—the recently discovered paradise was the river-region in Southern Chile. They also organized fishing trips, although half of their conversation was spent complaining that the golden age of fishing in Mexico was over. They nostalgically named places like Pucuato, Sabaneta, Mata de Pinos, Río Frío, Temascaltepec, the Iturbide Dam, the Nevado de Toluca, the Brockman Dam . . . They described the pollution, the deforestation, the lack of knowledge about aquatic matters and fish by those who ran the parks—who, in order to resolve the problems of nutrition in rural communities, bred carp anywhere; they put bass where there was already trout, and bass ate the trout-fry and eggs (if the carp didn't get there first) although they didn't grow more than fifteen centimeters long because of the low temperature—but they didn't let themselves lose heart, they spoke about projects to save the rainbow trout and, in passing, the country. They were elitists, it never would have occurred to them to fish for catfish or carp, and many of them sought in Mexico something that might have resembled the Pyrenees or the French or Italian Alps. But Joaquín enjoyed their company and was a good fisherman.

On one occasion they went to the mountains in Puebla and since neither of them was accompanied by his family, Joaquín shared a hotel room with a doctor Rogelio Méndez, a gynecologist. At midnight Doctor Méndez woke up startled. Licenciado Ballesteros Landero had moved (dragged?) his bed—by itself very heavy—several meters, but, now, what was even more amazing, he was half lifting a dresser—a piece of colonial furniture, a meter-and-a-half in height, and made of very heavy wood—and moving it toward the door. Doctor Méndez realized that his friend was still sleeping; so he spoke to him very calmly and managed to convince him to return to his bed. There were no more surprises, but I believe that Joaquín had a better night than his room-mate. This was the same man who crossed himself after catching a trout, she thought. And who very delicately freed them from the hooks to release them again into the water if they were too small. After catching two—if such was his fortune—he put away his equipment, and continued walking along the river or the lake-shore, no longer fishing. On one occasion Joaquín commented to Lourdes, "I don't know when I feel happier: when I haven't caught anything, when I catch something or, afterward, when I'm just walking." The next morning, Joaquín didn't believe what Rogelio told him, and the two had a good laugh. Not with little effort they returned the furniture to the places they'd occupied before. Doctor Méndez, a discreet man, didn't mention the incident during breakfast, which they'd gotten up early for. He only shared this with Lourdes when she, Joaquín, the doctor's wife and the doctor were seated at the table in the house of the Ballesteros Landaus, after a few months had passed.

Lourdes told this to me now that Joaquín was dead. Her husband was capable of having destroyed everything and of having flung himself out the window with sufficient force to land right in the middle of the patio but despite that and everything, the idea was unacceptable. Joaquín had fallen on his back, with his eyes open. Very emotionally and without looking at me, Lourdes said that when Joaquín listened to someone attentively, he frequently closed his eyes. His favorite position for listening to music was lying on the sofa, face up, resting on a cushion, with his eyes closed. Did he close his eyes when they made love?

More than the death of her husband, what disturbed her was the possibility that he might have committed suicide. Death in the hands of others was a violence that was awful and unacceptable, a part of the bosses' break with the system, of the struggle between the transnational mafias and their enemies, of groups in power that fought over the remains. Lourdes, like Joaquín, was one of those who believed in the necessary and inevitable breakup of the PRI, in the greater participation and maturity of civil society. But suicide would mean that she didn't know her husband. It was asking oneself at what moment had the false steps begun. Attempting to relate everything to the private sphere seemed like a double violence to her.

That night I found Lourdes on her knees, crying, by her husband's body. The dog looked at us from the bushes, where he'd gone to hide his grief. I tried to console her, offered her my handkerchief and embraced her. There wasn't any need to act too hastily. I prepared a tea with brandy for her. We didn't touch Joaquín except for Lourdes's gesture of closing his eyes, and covering him with a blanket up to his chest. Later, I told her we should return to the studio, something she didn't want to do, and without touching anything, see if she recognized anything that looked strange to her. Everything was out of its usual place, but even so, she might notice something missing. When we went downstairs again, she told me that she hadn't found the plastic box with the diskettes. Then she called her friend, the lawyer Enrique Fuentes, and he took charge of speaking with the authorities.

The investigation lasted almost all night. That coincided with the preparations for the funeral, the necessity of notifying family members (except Gisela), the obituary notes ... They returned on two other occasions. They always examined all the garbage. They placed the objects not totally destroyed on one of the shelves that was still against the wall, and Lourdes saw between the objects the box with the diskettes. There was the same number of them as on the last night when Joaquín had gone downstairs with the box to the bedroom. They returned what they had(n't) taken away. Lourdes asked permission to remove some articles. They, in turn, asked permission to search the rest of the house and she refused. On her son's computer they saw that the diskettes narrated the life of her husband up to the point when he wrote about his most recent work inside the government, which he'd been dismissed from because of some articles he'd published. The discovery made them happy. They knew that what Joaquín had published was only a small sample of his research. When Lourdes returned to work, she knew that while she was researching the relations between the Church and the State during the Porfirio Díaz era, others were searching her house. But that ambivalence over the death of her husband— was it possible not to have seen the box of diskettes that first night?—became clear with the visit of the governor . . . , who kept looking for something.

Joaquín hadn't committed suicide. Maybe they believed, when they discovered the box of diskettes, that they now had what they were looking for, and killed the author before he could write what really interested them. Very bad *timing*. Now they were biting their nails. Their nervousness was understandable. Either the author had died and, together with him, any knowledge contrary to his enemies' interests or whatever possibility of testifying, or the evidence was already written, but they didn't know where to find it, or whom to ask. Everything indicated that Joaquín hadn't confided in anybody. They were waiting for a morning when some U.S. or European newspaper broke the news.

Lourdes had a feeling that the text would be found in the house. She went over room by room the plants, the patio, the front garden, the car, every place imaginable—nobody knew her house better than she. She did it three times. She returned to her bedroom and to the studio, which seemed the most obvious places to her, and because of that, the most probable. She sat on her bed and tried to retrace the days, weeks, before Joaquín's death.

She was on her way to a restaurant with a friend when it came to her that the noise she'd occasionally heard, without realizing it, was that of the electric typewriter. It was the first time she'd gone out with someone who wasn't a relative since Joaquín's death, but she pulled over and told her friend that she was very sorry but she had to go back immediately. She left her next to her car in the parking lot and returned home. The memory was auditory. Sometimes she'd thought she heard her husband speaking out loud or arguing with someone; when she concentrated, the voices disappeared and the phenomenon revealed itself as a mixture, in equal doses, of imagination and solitude. In general, the music was always playing with the volume turned down, so that if she shouted something to Joaquín, he could hear her.

This sound was different. It was a pecking noise she hadn't placed or given importance to, until the moment in the car when she recognized it as the sound of the keys of the typewriter that her husband hadn't used in years, and that he kept, Lourdes believed, for sentimental reasons. The pecking had begun and had become continuous for about two weeks before his death; it was accompanied by a subtle increase in the music's volume and an improvement in her husband's spirits, and the first mention of his getting to the end of his project. After a few days, she stopped hearing it.

She doesn't know if the manuscript exists or, in the case of his having transferred his most recent work onto the typewriter, if whoever was looking for it discovered it. She doubts that, since they returned after the first time when, as they left, they asked Lourdes to leave everything as it was, in order to return to look among the debris, with the pretext of finding evidence to discover who were the "authors" of such barbarism. The electric typewriter, and some paper items were on one of the shelves in the bathroom of the studio . . . objects that the thieves had apparently ignored. She went up to the studio. She entered the bathroom and, taking care to use toilet paper so she wouldn't leave fingerprints, searched the contents of the shelf. There was no manuscript. They'd moved the paper items, but without becoming more interested in them. Everything looked new, in the sense that it had never been used, the ribbons with their original wrapping, the correction fluid with its seal intact, the box of paperclips full, the rubber-bands in the decorated can that their son Claudio had made. There wasn't paper; if it had existed they'd taken it away or destroyed it. They'd taken off the typewriter's cover.

Lourdes returned to her bedroom. She didn't eat. She slept out of discouragement. When she woke it was already night. She turned on the lamp and kept looking at the Latin characters between the medieval figures of angels on the shade. The writing might be on the ribbons and not on the paper! She only had to read the ribbons in reverse and everything would be there. She decided to wait until the next morning. She asked me in person to run an errand; fortunately, that day we were both at the university and she could approach me naturally in the hall. I used a visit to my parents in Morelia as a pretext to leave Mexico City in order to look for the ribbons she was asking me about.

It was an article that wouldn't be easy to find but neither would it be impossible. How many government databases are we not included in? How many organizations don't have a file with our name and personal information? How much of our correspondence—our telephone calls, our telegrams, our bank accounts and the activity of our credit cards (if we have them)—isn't intercepted and scrutinized routinely? But to be sure, I was under less surveillance than my friend.

What Lourdes feared most that weekend—since she must have been waiting for my usual visit on Monday afternoon at tea-time for us to see each other—was that someone might arrive and take away the ribbons. Everything had to appear normal so as not to involve more people and so that the investigation wouldn't continue. I visited her on Monday, and instead of MacMa cookies in a paper bag, I delivered the ribbons to her. She was euphoric, she laughed like a girl, it was the least ceremonious and shortest tea-time I remember at the Ballesteros Landau house, and she didn't open the bag until after I'd gone, although she did have a look and tears came to her eyes.

"They're identical," she said.

Using gloves, she placed the new ribbons in the exact place from which she'd taken the others. She returned to her bedroom. Joaquín had taken out the ribbons from the cellophane package, carefully opening one end. He'd typed on the ribbons, leaving a blank space at the beginning and end, he'd rewound them, returned them to their packages, and using heat, resealed them, although Lourdes didn't know how. Lourdes only had to open one of the ribbons with the same care and advance it a little in order to realize that it was full of writing. She couldn't sleep from emotion. Or better, from the emotions she'd discovered. On the one hand, happiness, the liberation of knowing that what her husband had done had some meaning. It confirmed, again, the intelligence and courage of the man she loved. On the other hand, the characters had seemed profound and persuasive forms of oppression to her, and so, for the moment, she hadn't wanted to read the contents.

The next day, through a common friend, she sent me the package. She didn't want to carry it to her own cubicle, because she knew they'd searched it and would continue doing so. Lourdes trusted that her friend, also her husband's friend for many years, would know how to retrieve the testimony in order to publish it afterwards, first marginally, as a note, so that later the major press could pick it up. It would shake the system (yet again) and would surely encourage the fall of the governor. . . and put an end to his political career.

From what location should one carry out betrayal? Ballesteros wanted a solitary retirement and wisely chose the roof of his own house. To make oneself incommunicado there isn't any better place; like a sheik, behind the garden, the terrace, the harem, in a central place but as if he had never stopped wandering on horseback through the mountains and the deserts.

This is what I thought to myself. I commented to Lourdes that we don't know who is governing us but we do know that for the most part they're perverse and that we, the ones who are governed, are for the most part neurotic—a very unfortunate combination. She thought that, even considering everything that had happened, I was painting a too-catastrophic scenario. That night she entered the studio, after stopping at the foot of the stairs and calling him to come down for dinner, without getting a response. The German Shepherd wasn't lying down in front of the door as was usual at that hour, either. She entered fearfully and immediately felt the cold and the air from the broken big window. She crossed the debris, sensing that her husband was no longer in the room. She walked to the far wall of the room, stopped in front of the space that the window had occupied, marked by jagged and sharp pieces of glass, and looked toward the patio because the German Shepherd was watching her. His yellow eyes like two points of light. Enormous, still fireflies. They stared at each other for what seemed a long time, and then she followed the gaze of the dog, who'd tilted his head, until she came upon the prone figure of her husband. That was when she screamed.

The ribbons contain what Lourdes suspected: a testimony at once impassioned and intelligent, about the corrupt government of ____. Logical but like a dog that doesn't stop gnawing at a bone. He expresses himself as he was, finally, a journalist, notwithstanding his political career and as a man of letters. He thought that now, with grown sons, he could leave her alone. Something I haven't done. I go to the Ballesteros Landau home often. The dog doesn't bark at me, he doesn't mistrust me. They say that dogs can tell who are the real friends of their masters. He wags his tail, like always. Lourdes doesn't understand the delay. I tell her not to despair, that it's a matter of patience.

The Dwarf Bull

to José Blanco Regueira

Juan came to the conclusion, although he didn't share it with either Diego or Concha, that they were wrong. The bull was a bull. He didn't require mystery or a labyrinth. He receded down the street and when he'd gone fifteen or more steps he'd stop so they could follow him, even if Concha raised her arms and shouted, in a tone that tried to sound affectionate and firm at the same time, for him to keep moving.

"Go, Chino!"

When the dwarf bull returned, Concha would kneel and embrace him. After she stroked him between his little horns, they'd continue walking.

How is he ever going to move, thought Juan.

Concha became emotional on two separate occasions: when for a moment the bull no longer looked back, and when he'd returned to her. Concha had no interest in middle distances. Juan actually said it once, as the three of them stood on some street corner:

"Poor thing! You're both robbing him of any initiative. He moves and we remain here, not following him."

He was going to add "immobile," but it wasn't true. Concha never stopped moving, although at times her movements might be very slow. She danced as if they were attached by a very long thread, an invisible, slender leash, perhaps, that stretched thinner as the animal drew away from them. It was the deliberate steps of the bull that set her into motion.

"Did you say he's your cousin?" Concha asked Diego.

"I wouldn't swear to it," Diego said.

"You bastard," said Juan, and lit a cigarette.

"They don't like smoke," Concha said.

"Let's pretend it's incense," said Juan, and it seemed to him as if Concha smiled before turning away.

Diego took a cigarette from him and Juan lit it.

"Thanks, cousin," Diego said.

"You're welcome."

Concha had put a collar on him made of blue fabric, knotting a slender cord, no more than two meters long, through its small ring. The little ritual, carried out in the middle of the biggest room, put an end to the exhibition more clearly than if Diego had asked his visitors to leave. When only the three of them remained, it was necessary for Diego to introduce Juan to Concha, since it was obvious that she thought he would also be leaving.

"The change doesn't seem to bother him," said Concha, looking at the bull.

Juan asked himself how she was thinking of getting him down to the street. His legs were very short for the heftiness of his body, and if the animal tried to descend by the stairs, it was obvious he'd fall flat on his face and break his neck. When he made that remark to Concha, she looked at him with such haughtiness and contempt that Juan felt she wasn't as much out of his reach as she might have seemed, and he felt flattered, even if there wasn't a hint of flattery in Concha's response: she told him that Chino wasn't the one with four legs and a snout, and if someone was going to fall down the stairs, it would be Juan, who despite having his eyes completely open, was as blind as a post.

Nobody laughed, so Juan held back his laughter.

"He weighs an awful lot," Diego told him. "Can you give me a hand?"

He had to demonstrate even more self-control so as not to break out laughing when he realized that Diego was joking, since the bull would be traveling on an elevator platform that ran along the banister from the second to the ground floor.

"That was the reason I bought the apartment," Diego told him, partly conceding his ignorance. "As a sculptor, it seemed to be an ideal appliance for me. It was installed by the son of the previous landlady, an old woman who no longer could go up or down stairs. There used to be a seat on the elevator."

The dwarf bull had ridden the elevator his entire brief life. It was the only conceivable way for him to go up to or down from the apartment. Diego let his neighbors use the elevator to bring up groceries or some heavy object. Except for that, Diego didn't have much to do with them or vice-versa.

"Concha? She's an actress," he said earlier that same night, when Juan accompanied him to open more bottles of wine, and asked him about the woman with the blue dress and the green diadem decorated with all kinds of multicolored animals.

"Before that, she was a dancer but she messed up her knee." Diego didn't have furniture. Or if he had any, he distributed it among his friends when he needed space in his apartment to create and exhibit his sculptures. Now, all his belongings were in the kitchen. His clothing in a corner of the cupboard. His toothbrush, razor and soap next to the sink, because the dwarf bull slept in the bathroom, where he also spent most of the day, the room spacious, with big windows and good light, and a plank-wood floor that somewhat softened the impact of his hooves. He was a thick, massive animal, and given his bulk, one wouldn't have expected him to be so light-footed. Diego put straw and his other food in the tub, which also served as a trough for the bull. At first, he'd drunk from the toilet bowl, but now he didn't go near it. Perhaps because he'd grown, not so much as to prevent him from drinking from it, but enough so that it would be difficult for him to do, given the size of his head and the lateral position of his eyes. Another possibility also occurred to Diego: the noise frightened him. Concha didn't agree. For her, Chino was afraid of the toilet because of his knowledge of labyrinths. The bowl was the entrance to the complicated network of pipes that we no longer perceive because of our enormous capacity to hide everything below the surface.

Diego had forgotten why he'd gone into the kitchen and, holding the open wine-bottle in his hand, took out two glasses and sat down in a chair—the only one—next to the table, gesturing to Juan to sit on the cot. Juan sat beneath the clothing hanging from a wire and they toasted the family, although it had been years since Diego had seen most of them. When they invited him to weddings, he'd send one of his sculptures as a gift. Few of them appreciated his art, but he didn't care. Once an exhibition was over, he was the first one to deny that what remained had any value. Whatever wasn't picked up by friends or gallery owners, was left for the garbage-truck.

Concha was an old friend of his. At one time they'd been intimate. But now, Diego confided to him, she seemed, above all, more interested in the bull.

Although he'd put an end to their love relationship, now he wanted to be with her again, to make love to her. Concha told him that that would be impossible as long as Chino was with them. It could even be dangerous.

Even before then, during the period when he was preparing his exhibition, he would walk the dwarf bull. They went out at night to avoid dogs—in general they reacted with fear: they probably imagined he was a big dog that didn't bark—and pedestrians, who became indignant, above all when the dwarf bull stopped to defecate or urinate. They walked for hours through the streets of Colonia Condesa and Colonia Roma, a pastime both truly enjoyed. He was extraordinarily tame, and Diego had put a leash on him only because two patrolmen had demanded it. He took it off whenever he could so the bull could nibble grass and drink from the fountains.

"You look happy," said Juan.

"Yes, it's true. I wait for everyone to leave so I can go out with Concha and Chino."

She insisted that Chino wasn't just any animal. On one occasion, Diego was talking to him about the nightly walks as Concha, to pass the time, studied a map of Colonia Condesa on the wall—with a red circle indicating where the apartment was located, plus some writing, also done with a red magic marker, *You are here*—and she said that Chino was looking for a way to return to his own world, which was joined to ours by a labyrinth. She liked to recreate myths. She'd always been obsessed with the journey of Theseus, the image of the black sails departing and returning.

Juan never knew when to take Diego and his friends seriously.

"She's kept what matters, don't you see? The bull, the girl, the young man. . . ."

151

Diego had more than enough women. Juan had confirmed it again that same night. They followed him through the galleries of the exhibition, they surrounded him, it seemed like a fashion show in which the same three or four women changed outfits every twenty or thirty minutes.

"I'm lucky, I know it," said Diego. "It's something inexplicable, gratuitous, it's probably hormonal . . . But I'll tell you something: the only woman who interests me now is Concha." She was accompanying the bull, who also was roaming through the exhibition. Their couple-like behavior also seemed to make them inaccessible, or invisible, to the others. It was strange that most of them weren't amazed by the animal (who was himself gorgeous—an unusual combination of strength and tenderness, the healthy sheen of his pelt, the enormous, clear eyes, dark brown and tranquil—but also powerful, the size of his head, the little horns, the hooves that made a sound—a slight vibration, like a big drum—with every step, the testicles no longer a calf's) or the admirable woman who accompanied him, tall with black, curly hair similar to her eyes, so dark they seemed to be all pupil, her thick eyebrows and long eyelashes equally dark in contrast with her white skin and her lips, neither fleshy nor deep red, but a color marked by its uniqueness. He also realized, not without sadness, that what had looked to him like distance, or lack of interest, between Diego and the woman wasn't that. The thought came to him that women who look like they're alone rarely are.

"She always comes to my exhibitions," continued Diego. "I like that because she doesn't insist on interpreting what I do. She'd often laugh. 'You're really crazy,' she used to tell me. But all that's changed.

"She returned to the map and studied it as if she could discover in the layout of its streets and parks some clue, something that might indicate a mistake in the plan. She decided, after numerous failed attempts, that the only way to do that was to go for a walk. 'The meaning of turning a corner,' she told me, pointing to some of the almost infinite possibilities on the map, 'is that turning implies a change, specifically, of direction, to get one's bearings another way, to discover another meaning of space, to shift direction. . . .' I feared that she was the one who even before then was shifting direction, and not for her own good."

The torn-up knee had made her appreciate what it means to walk differently, to change the way one dances, to balance one's weight on the feet. The additional weight looked good on her; before that, she'd appeared too thin to Diego. But Concha wasn't an actress, and for her to try to stop dancing at her age in order to learn, almost from scratch, another art, surely wasn't only disturbing for her, but would also seem reckless.

We should see this, she'd said, passing her hand over the map, as a topography of turns. We'll walk in a straight line, in one direction, then in the opposite direction, as if in reality we were moving neither forward nor backward, as Chino chooses the street that will be his shortcut.

When Juan arrived at his cousin's exhibition, he didn't know what to expect. The sculptor was dressed all in leather. He was walking with a dwarf bull at his side. The animal, Diego explained to his cousin, had been born on the ranch of a painter friend's relatives and on a visit there, Diego became fond of him. Diego asked them to sell him the animal instead of slaughtering him. He had curly fur, like little snails, all over his head, and the rest of his body looked like a fabric wrinkled by the tautness of its nap. He was a Hereford, with white eyelashes and a light brown body. They laughed at Diego and then his friend insisted on giving him the bull as a gift.

Diego chatted with his guests, above all with the women, he offered them more wine, and when the bull defecated, he placed a sign next to it that said: *the great turd of the dwarf bull*. When he urinated he had another sign, in a different color: *the dwarf bull's urine*. In the latter case, he headed toward the bathroom for a bucket and mop and cleaned everything up so that the visitors didn't slip or get their shoes dirty. Diego was pleased because he'd been able to use both signs that night. He explained to them that fecal material and urine were used in different ways to cure leather. It was only when a woman arrived, kissing Diego on both cheeks after doing the same to the bull as she exclaimed "You're divine!," that the animal stopped following his master and stayed with her.

Juan took advantage of this to view the exhibition. It was organized as multiple scenes. The first one had two hospital beds, with very thin mattresses from an earlier time, it seemed, because they measured a meter and 60 centimeters at most. The bedclothes, old but very clean and white; the beds expertly made, the pillows placed on the folded sheet. The frames, heads and feet were made of thin iron with a matte finish; it seemed as if the sculptor, in order to remove all dirt and mold, had worked the surfaces with a brush made of metal bristles. The strange thing about the bedroom—if one could call it that—was that one of the beds was set at a normal height and the other was raised— the feet were like stilts—almost two meters above the floor, in such a way that it came very close to the ceiling, and one could see, from underneath, the white metal bars of the frame like some animal's ribs. In order to separate the two beds from each other, the sculptor had placed between them a screen made of a fine white hide, tied by a cord to a tubular frame, placed vertically on wheels. The effect was comic and absurd, laughable and sad at the same time. That artifact, which attempted to provide each of the patients with his own space, however minimal, through the different heights of the two beds, left them completely uncovered, although in order to look at each other one of them would have to turn completely face-up, and the other one face-down. The one on top could remain quiet and almost hidden, but the moment he appeared he would also be seen, even if it were only his face. It wasn't the only thing in the room. There were few objects in relation to the space they took up, which minimized and isolated them. A round-metal table with a glossy finish that reflected everything was placed at the foot of the lower bed. On top of it were a doctor's or surgical instruments, also made of metal, a syringe, scissors, a few scalpels, some pairs of forceps, different kinds of tweezers, needles—among them one ready for sewing cloth with white thread—and some instruments with no reason for being there—a hole-punch, a stapler, a scraper, a knife . . . tools out of a stationery store for working leather—but, given their dated nature and the material they were made of, they didn't draw attention to themselves, unless one looked closely. The table-top was placed on a threaded base, with three legs that also ended in wheels. It was, if one concentrated on the lower part instead of its shiny surface, actually a stool, the kind that's rotated to raise or lower it, very common at one time.

Aside from the table-stool, the only other object was a cradle, similar in construction to the beds, with an equally thin mattress, the same scrubbed finish but severe when one looked at it, with the same bedclothes although the pillow was smaller in size. Each of the four legs rested on a child's white leather shoe. One looked like a little girl's.

Juan then moved on—it didn't seem important to follow a set path—to a small entrance hall where, at first glance, everything looked almost normal. The coat-rack, the sofa, the end-table, the lamp and the rug. Two things seemed strange to him: the first was his awareness that everything was made of hide. The jacket hanging up was made of leather, as was the twin sofa. The end-table looked like a bongo, with its tight hide cover and cylindrical wooden base, and the lampshade was made of a fine translucent hide. The rug was made of a horse's hide, with mane and tail. The second thing that seemed strange to him was that the two pillows on the sofa, also made of hide, were, on closer observation, made from unborn bulls. They looked like toys, or animal crackers.

He'd reached his cousin, who, for a moment, found himself alone.

"Where did you get these things?" he asked as if amused, although he felt repugnance.

"I make them," said Diego, "with materials I find abandoned in garbage dumps or that I buy from trash-pickers or in some thrift shop."

"But that," said Juan, pointing to the pillows.

"I found them in a furrier's shop."

"But are they real or did you cut and sew the pieces?"

"Look closely and tell me yourself."

"I prefer not to."

"Cows also abort. They're fetuses. And there's no reason to be alarmed by the rug. It belonged to a gentleman who in this way preserved the memory of those creatures that, while they were alive, seemed like an extension of himself. There wasn't a pastime that he liked more than riding. Or that's what his heirs told us when they sold the hacienda to have it divided up. Keep enjoying yourself, I'm going for more wine. Have you tried it? I'll bring you a glass. Why don't you sit down?"

Juan kept standing but he waited, obediently, without changing his spot. Between the hospital room and the *estancia*, he really wouldn't know which to choose and he would have preferred to go outside under the pretext of smoking a cigarette.

The woman who'd been with the bull arrived and handed him a glass of white wine, although she wasn't drinking. They both remained silent and he tried the wine. He said that he was thinking of going out for a moment for a smoke and she told him it wasn't necessary to leave, that in case he hadn't noticed, almost everyone was smoking and if he wanted to put out his cigarette, he could do it on any surface there. There wasn't a lack of ashtrays. It didn't bother Diego, in fact he himself had set the example, and she showed him various places, on the sofa, on the table, on one of the cushions. . . . The woman looked like an actress. She spoke her lines very well, and before leaving, invited Juan to proceed into the next room, since he shouldn't stay exclusively in the receiving area although they left in the opposite direction.

He entered and all around him the same object was repeated, but made of different materials. They were casts of the sculptor's body. The first one, predictably, was made of plaster—its whiteness picked up the whiteness of the hospital room—in two halves that had been placed, open, on the floor as if the sculptor had been deprived of a thicker skin. Juan remembered when they'd removed his plaster cast the same way, using an electric saw, and how slender and discolored his leg looked. The front half, face-down, had small holes one could imagine he'd breathed through. There was also a profile of an entire body made of leather stretched onto a frame similar to the screen between beds. Then, joining two hides, like he'd done with the two calf fetuses, the sculptor had made a mannequin that was a replica of himself. He'd also used different materials, chosen from among what one finds in any house—aluminum foil, melted plastic, cardboard, old rags, newsprint, cellophane, shattered glass and ceramic. . . everything flammable, ephemeral, brittle or sharp— to create casts, which looked like funeral masks, but of different parts of his body, and had placed the pieces throughout the room, as if the repetition of his form were endless. Juan thought that the only thing missing was for him to lie down naked on the wooden floor in the middle of his visitors. He commented that to the woman, who'd once again approached him.

"It's exactly what most of them are waiting for," she said, without hiding her distaste. "Then they'll follow his example. But according to the logic of this room, what you're suggesting is impossible."

Juan looked around.

"I don't understand. Why?"

"He would have to lie down simultaneously face-up and face-down. And it's impossible for him to do that, don't you think?"

"I hadn't thought of that, but it's true. He must have told you that."

"No way! Those things never occur to him. He's a child. Or, if he isn't, he hides his thoughts very well, or he keeps them to himself. If I were to make the same observation right now and he heard me, it would ruin the evening for him. He's kind-hearted, Diego is. According to him, this exhibition isn't about him, but about Chino."

And she looked at the bull.

He had no reason not to arrive. He'd thought that at the beginning of the evening, and now he again began losing himself among the streets of Colonia Condesa. And it wasn't the first time he'd gotten lost on the way to his cousin's apartment. In general, he didn't get lost, but there was something about those streets that made them devilishly difficult.

When he said goodbye to them, he thought of returning immediately to the house where he was staying. But he didn't know where he'd parked his car and he couldn't get his bearings, either. He looked at his watch; it was a few minutes before four. Out of pride, he didn't want to return to them; but even if he'd wanted that, with their movement, and his too, and now being lost, the chance of finding them was extremely slim. He'd already walked for many blocks. When he decided he was lost, he began to walk in a straight line so he could cross some avenue. For a few moments he'd follow the headlights of some vehicle, but few passed by and then receded from view. He didn't try to stop them, either. He didn't see any taxis. He ended up breaking into laughter. He sat down on a bench. It was a recognizable object. During the day, couples in love sat there. A thought that was preceded and accompanied by Concha's image. He'd wait for the dawn. He told himself that at night it's better to stay in one place or to leave in someone else's company.

Vasari, Do You Hear Me?

to Larry D. Bouchard and Peggy Galloway

*At last, the Supreme Maker decided that this creature
(man before the Fall), to whom He could give nothing
wholly his own, should have a share in the particular
endowment of every creature.*

—PICO DE LA MIRANDOLLA,

ORATION ON THE DIGNITY OF MAN

Love makes the body

—JEAN-LUC MARION

What to do with Jesus Christ? Copy what the ancients did, what
some continue doing, and so free myself from obstacles and
problems that rob me of my sleep and alter my humors, making
me irritable and melancholy? Those who'd be pleased by such
a turn in my affairs aren't few. Oh, they'd say, Master Da Vinci
finally completes what he begins, he carries out what's asked of
him without pondering it so much. But must I please courte-
sans, who think with the rings on their fingers and the softness
of their beards, or religious men, who trade in Jesus Christ even

more than Florentines do with cloth, dyes, or spices, or certain painters—not to scandalize them—who paint only because they believe they know how to do that and nothing else? I know the number of bones in a man—and I don't believe that they vary from man to man or from man to woman—but if religious men could suggest, and be convincing, that Jesus Christ's body had three or seven times as many bones as any other man, they would do so. If they succeeded, since this also holds true for saints, the business for relics would be more profitable than for cloth, and the Florentine bourgeoisie would wear habits. But I'm sure that if I were to open the body of Jesus Christ, I'd find nothing different inside it. When I imagine him, I give him the best attributes I've seen in countless faces I've contemplated over a life that now seems too long to me. Even so, I hold on to many pieces, and I look at him when I close my eyes, and I don't see him, but I do see the nose and forehead of ___, the eyebrows of ___, the chin of ___, the waist of ___—even worse, at times his attributes have been taken from cadavers, or from people I find nasty because of their cruelty or malice or because they've wished me some harm and plot against me. How to take from what's dead and give expression to what's most alive? How to pretend that an individual man might look like him? How to paint him, then, as I've always done, observing what surrounds me, what I see when I squint or close my eyes? Where to find him? In caves, among tree-branches, in rock-crevices, in flowing water and its whirl-pools, in the distant hills and sky, in the inner world of sleep or of twilight sleep, between the world of adults and that of children, in the sunny world or in a bedroom or workshop largely closed to sunlight and outside noise?

Placing him where he should go wasn't a problem: in the center of all axes. I didn't choose the spot, as some say, because

162

of the light coming through the window on the opposite wall, although this seemed to me, from the beginning, more an omen than coincidence. An omen, although I might not have known it then, of the impossible task I'd proposed for myself. That light, as long as the window and the wall exist, will illuminate the same spot. It's obvious that sunlight will survive an artisan's pigments. I find it in many places, even without seeking it, but I haven't found *him*. Maybe I don't know what it is I'm painting. I try but now and then I prefer to stop. I'm able to paint him as a child. Is it because he didn't have a father? Could he have become an adult as the son of God any other way? Joseph was a guardian more than a father; when Jesus Christ was very young, Joseph was already a disciple of his own son. He had two fathers. The two natures of Christ are like the two natures of his relationship with his father, Joseph. He was and wasn't his father. Joseph had a wife who wasn't a wife and a son who also wasn't his in the human sense. The Holy Spirit had a wife but only visited her once, and the company he kept with her, like with Jesus Christ, was mysterious and, so it would seem, distant. Mary had various suitors besides Joseph, but they were angels. They're the only ones who appear in paintings. Mary didn't know man but was the wife of the Holy Spirit, the mother of Jesus, and for many years the companion of Joseph. In her gestures toward Joseph, she's more sister than woman, in her relationship with the Holy Spirit, she's more of a girl, loving and obedient, than a wife, but in her relationship with Jesus she never stops treating him like a son. It must be a little strange that there are so many paintings of Madonnas with the infant Jesus. How to include Joseph, if he's not herding an ass? And the Holy Spirit, who, as his name signifies, is holy and spirit? Or Jesus Christ at 33 years of age? I don't like crucifixions.

Very well. I'm not going to look in nature—because he isn't there—or in my mind—because he isn't there—in order to be able to paint him on a wall, where he isn't either, and that's the problem. Trying to draw his face with what I have at hand doesn't work because I have it at hand, it doesn't matter how I readjust it, it's not revealed to me. The body in the fresco is no more than clothes, the knowledge of fabrics and of how to cover a man. The hands and their position come from various Milanese men and not any single one, they're the fruit of thousands of sketches; the legs are hidden by the cloth, and the cloth falls around a seated figure very similarly from one man to the next. But the feet! It's true, most men never look closely at feet unless they're amputated or have problems walking, or they're kissed by someone—out of desire or obligation. They're almost as difficult as hands. I've noticed, in public baths, that feet reveal much about an individual's nature. In hospitals and morgues, the feet also show what a person's life has been like and, sometimes, the maladies he suffers or has suffered. The neck is drawn at the same time as the head.

I have to guess not if Jesus is a man, but his divinity. I can frighten my friends with a tame, disguised lizard, but I can't give Jesus a face. What's communicated in an instant is a whole. The parts are all real and recognizable but, at the same time, how to say it?, we have the sensation of facing something that shouldn't be but truly is. Although in a way we hadn't known. And it's not a theatrical effect or an ingenious disguise. I think about something that will explode in my friends' minds but differently than their response to my lizard mascot. Not as a joke. I can't work with the Deity as I have with the lizard. The lizard is a visual image, apart from being a lizard bejeweled and dressed for a ball: it's a mental image that's become tangible: it's a toy, a hand-made artifact that's become visible and an image. I know the origin, or origins, of what I've created, as with entertainments at court. In reality, one doesn't create the origin but indeed the origins out of what already exists. But what creator tries to recreate the Creator? I'm amazed before nature, before its wonders, but I come out of my lethargy, I'm immobile but the malady is temporary. Because all immobility is a malady. There isn't an absolute immobility. The movement of cadavers is much less than that of the living. When it's difficult for me to rise in the morning, I pretend I'm dead until I leap up with a bound.

It's not that he may be of a different race. Neither is it pretending that the wall might become paint and the paint a human being, nor transforming something without recognizing it, as if Jesus Christ could be the same as any of his disciples. What a horror if someone contemplated the work and pointed to another of the figures and said: "How well Master Da Vinci has executed the image of Jesus Christ!" Or worse if someone asked: "And which of all of them, for the love of God, is Jesus Christ?" So that the question became: can you finish what's missing with what you have?

What happened with the ancients, or happens with some of my contemporaries, who never know if they're before a man, an animal, or a God, doesn't occur with me. I don't want to perceive more there than what might show me a truth about what I've painted, just as when I draw a cat, the gestures, the posture, the features, the proportions, all the details show me it's a cat and not something else. But no one would be so foolish as to confuse that cat with one that boys chase after or that's seated on the window-sill taking the sun. I want to paint Jesus Christ as Jesus Christ, so no one confuses him with someone he isn't. But now I don't have him before me as indeed I had___ or ___. I don't

165

have the good fortune of the apostles or the first disciples. If one paints the Virgin taking the best of what one finds in mothers, one should be able to do the same thing with her son: to paint Jesus Christ with the best of what one finds in men. But I've failed. Why is it easier for me to paint angels? To do so, I use the beauty of young men or children, and birds—not any bird, not any winged creature. Where is depth hidden? On the surface. I've opened the belly of a pregnant woman's cadaver, but I've discovered more answers to Life's enigma in a young pregnant woman who's posed for me. Which is not to deny the wonder of that little man wrapped, in candle-light, in the walls of his mother. Beneath that fragility there was a structure, forms inside of others that had nothing to do with what had already died. Oh, wonderful prodigy of the Supreme Master! When I left the morgue, it was on the verge of dawn and I felt ecstatic. It's common to place bats' wings on demons, although these creatures also have their strange grace, one only has to see them exiting caves at evening to hunt insects or sip water from pools, or their bone-structure and the membrane of their wings that fold very differently from those of birds. One must know with the eyes and the hand. The eye passes over a creature without the need to capture it. But the hand needs to touch what it observes before painting it. Have I ever touched Jesus Christ or rested my head on his chest? Even those who took him down from the cross and prepared him for burial knew him in a very different and superior way to mine. A blind man who hasn't been so for part of his life perceives differently than a man blind from birth. A blind man who passes his hand over a beloved's features and body knows differently than a man who sees but doesn't know how to touch. Who hasn't met different creatures when he dreams? But

166

I want to paint The Last Supper and not the apostles asleep on the night of Gethsemane.

One can study human monsters and look for a way to explain the origin, the cause, of their deformity, or want to explain, according to what one already knows, those unusual creatures described by travelers, not unreal or non-existent because they're different and unknown in our lands, since nature's variety seems limitless, creatures that will be revealed as belonging to some feverish sailor or are the inventions of those who like to deceive with the products of their own imaginations, or of lying necromancers, or are creatures who belong to treatises known under the name of demonologies. . . they'll be discovered again or will forever remain creatures of the imagination or will keep waiting for a new encounter. I know when the fantastic imitates nature, the guesswork of discovering what's only revealed to the sight with patient and fixed attention, the metamorphosis of creatures and the different stages of their transformation, the constancy of forms and the infinite variations that can be created from them. Creating outside the borders of nature is impossible. One must observe attentively, even what occurs in dreams. But Jesus Christ isn't a composition in this sense, a change of elements, a rapid transition; nevertheless, still being new from the beginning, there's nothing fantastic about him, but who would say that he isn't extraordinary? I follow the masters in whatever I can learn from them; I follow nature more, to which I apply art, nature, where the ambiguous, the undefined, the still non-existent, mystery, but not the fantastic, exist.

But Jesus, who is no different from man, according to the senses, what must one do to give him form? All of him, his gestures, his physique, his emotions, his words, his clothing, is taken from man, but they lack the malice, the cruelty, the lies, the hypocrisy . . . so that with less than man, he is more and better than him. I know how to draw what's more, but how to do it with what's less? I don't try to explain it. That would be very daring! It's the job of illustrious men, those who know about Godly things. And by illustrious men, I'm not referring to the Prior of Santa Maria delle Grazie, who looks more like a sea monster with a monk's head that appears in the book of monsters and wonders. If he mortified himself only a tenth of what he does to me, he'd be a saint already. He believes that the head of my Christ is going to emerge from the torso—which is no more than cloth with some folds—like a cabbage from the earth of his vegetable garden. He should dedicate himself to the latter, it's more secure and for him, I have no doubt, ultimately more gratifying. Maybe at bottom, he's no more than a simple man who means well, and the headless figures of Judas and Jesus Christ perturb him differently than they do me. Why doesn't he say anything about the other eleven figures? Jesus Christ has an advantage over Judas, he has hands while the traitor hasn't gotten any yet. And betraying requires hands or lips and a tongue—feet aren't enough. He's surely simple, but why did God make him so stubborn?

My patron is also demanding but in an intelligent and astute way, he's often cruel and hardly rational, but his unpredictability makes him interesting. Besides, he has a good sense of humor. To create monsters and wonders it's only necessary to live for a while in the company of men. Many creatures presented in those manuals whose drawings we study perhaps aren't fantastic and we'll recognize them, since they'll still look the same when, sooner or later, the Flood comes.

Wandering around is one of the activities I like best. To be moving and thinking about a thousand things. They complain that I'm impatient, they complain that I delay too much. That I don't finish things. When I walk I'm patient. I enjoy moments of laziness. Having no task, no assignment to carry out by a certain date. I get lost in parts of the city where no one knows me, where whoever looks at me considers me as strange as I do them. The opposite of life at court where one must be friendly even with the walls and eloquent even with the deaf. When I no longer desire to escape the vortex of what awaits me, without caring how vain the effort, I leave the studio for the street, the market, the public baths . . . where everything multiplies and disperses and I gather a small part of it in my notebooks, or when I feel too lethargic, I only observe. I know that it's time to return when what I observe overwhelms me, or when some details serve my work and the world of men stops interesting me. The vision of what intrigues me is more real than shouts, noises, brushing against people.

I also like tales. Writing, as well. If I'd had more of an education, maybe I would have written more. It's not true that I didn't paint Christ's face. I left Judas for last. The prior entered when I'd finished everything except the traitor's face. He didn't react. He glanced at the fresco, from left to right, as if he were reading something that didn't interest him. So much work for an unworthy wall! When man eats he doesn't pay attention; his gaze is fixed on the plate of lentils in front of him.

"And why haven't you painted that one?" was the only thing he asked, after pestering me so much. It made me so angry that I decided to carry out my threat and adopt the physical features of this prior who has complained several times about me before Your Excellency and who, given the failure of my inquiries elsewhere, isn't such a bad model. *It no longer was him, but how was I going to convince him? He saw himself in that portrait, I saw something for which a fleeting gesture of ___was the most import-*

ant thing. Painting diminished my anger, and the prior became one
of multiple inspirations. I'd hesitate in making him look ridiculous
before his whole convent. My Judas was the very image of the Prior
of the Dominicans of Santa Maria delle Grazie.

He erased Christ. Then he boasted that I'd repented my
wrongdoing, because Judas immediately began to lose form.

"I haven't touched the fresco," I said, when confronted with
his comment that I never left things in peace. The prior looked
at me mockingly.

"Just as I haven't touched your Christ."

"There are two possible explanations, Your Excellency," I
subsequently responded to the duke. "Whoever erased Christ
immediately erased Judas."

"And the second explanation?" he asked me.

"Judas, not having anyone to look at, vanished."

The duke burst into laughter at what he called my ingenuity.
Judas, not having anyone to look at, vanished. Christ was his life
as much as he was the life of the other disciples. The things that
amused my patron surprised me at times. For me, the work was
finished. I asked permission to take leave and I walked through
the solitary hall. It occurred to me that I was the motive for the
prior's sinning. Later, my pride was such that I said the figures
crumbled because I'd gone away and worked on something else.

The above is a fabrication. It's true that I left the heads of
Judas and Jesus Christ unfinished for a long time. Somehow,
Judas was placed right where I was going to need him later. I
knew from the start that he should look as if he were getting
up from that side of the table, close to Christ, because only he
who is close by can betray. The other apostles were finished and
through their gestures and postures effectively expressed the
emotions I'd wanted to attribute to them and, if one can speak

of splendor regarding human poverty, they were dignified and noble figures, men whom one could trust. Everyone reacted differently but according to their nature. The relation of the forms to each other was appropriate, the depths conforming to perspective, the focus on the one who was still absent, but it's also true that the viewer's attention would be drawn to the figure just to the left (for the viewer, to the right) of Jesus Christ. There was now a certain violence in it since, although forming part of one of the four triads, it seemed out of place from the whole group. An effect owing, perhaps, to the rotation of its shoulders and its closeness to Jesus Christ, which more than loving, seemed threatening. I knew in an instant of contemplation that Judas, who still didn't have arms, wanted to touch Our Lord. Painting his hand extended was an immediate and firm reaction, the open hand that wants to grasp but still doesn't touch what it seeks, a gesture I've seen innumerable times, in innumerable men, in innumerable situations. A scandalous, threatening gesture, of something that's taken and, almost at the same moment, refused, or a movement of someone who's checked the opposite impulse, a gesture full of ambiguity, of duplicity, of someone who doesn't belong to himself, or who's lost control, exhibiting an illicit desire that until that moment he's succeeded in keeping hidden. The other apostles react as one would expect after their master's question. Judas is the only one out of key, without being contrary to the counsel of reason and natural effects. Once the arms had been painted, I knew that—aside from the composition and perspective— it was Judas who emotionally focused the attention of anyone looking at the fresco on the Deity. Maybe it was also through the strange and sinister gaze of he who knew Christ but was thinking of betraying him that one could know who caused, without wanting to and surely with some pain, that

171

jumble of emotions in one of his disciples. Because the other apostles look outward, but Judas, while he is the one who looks most intensely at his Lord, also most clearly has an anxious gaze directed at his own soul. Perversely, but repeated again and again in nature, Judas, in his betrayal, was heading toward its opposite.

The only way to paint Judas was to see his reaction, his attitude, his gestures before Christ. I've seen scions before their lords, slaves before their masters, submissive women before their husbands. It was when I completed Judas's hands and arms that I understood I shouldn't be seeking his features but his gaze, since the way he looked at Jesus Christ would give away not only his own face but the face of the one he was going to betray.

I didn't go to certain places to look for Judas's face. That was a pretext. There was no place where I couldn't discover the type I was seeking now. I could also say that there wasn't a person in whom I sometimes couldn't discover what I sought. Every day I headed for the Borghetto, and to other places, in the morning and at night. I told everyone else—those who felt they had the right to question me about my affairs—that I was going to the spot where the ruffians, thieves, prostitutes, and pimps lived, to see if I could find models there for my Judas. I would offend them if I confided that I could discover that scoundrel without going too far. I look everywhere. Different faces can be revealed in a single man. It should cause them consternation, but most probably it would only outrage them to know the different origins of the apostles and, even more, of Judas. Masters whom I admire have told me I've made an enormous mistake trying to paint The Last Supper without relying more on tradition. They advise that I leave the fresco incomplete. That only God can complete it. That I quit. As if that were possible! At least the pretext of seeking Judas has given me a free hand to wander through the city on a whim, without anyone adding to the list, already very long, of my strange pastimes. Strangers have approached me in the street—I don't know how word got out—to tell me that they have some relative or friend who'd be perfect for what I'm seeking. How little they understand art! Of course, they're hoping for a few coins in return (how well they understand art). Sometimes I've gone with them because of my insatiable curiosity. On no few occasions, the trip has turned out to be valuable. Not, however, as far as finding Judas, who in the popular mind is a grotesque being, physically deformed. Everyone thinks he knows Judas. The sketches I did pleased the Moor, who shares with me a love of strange things.

One shouldn't wish for the impossible but I believed I'd discovered what I was seeking, and returned to the convent. I didn't leave until I'd finished the figure of the traitor, and it happened as I'd thought it would: I began the drawing of Christ that same day. As I completed the work, the other apostles, until that moment somehow disparate, became real, seated at the table, let me put it this way, to take up space in the refectory.

Now that the work was finished, I let some days pass. Out of superstition but also because the first comments I received were praiseworthy and I debated whether to trust in something so sweet to my ears, or to mistrust it, which was my first impulse, knowing that I was the best critic of my own work and harsher than any other man. As opposed to before I finished the fresco, when I received the observations and comments of numerous viewers and I showed equal interest with all, whether they were experts or chatterboxes, wise-men or fools, "personalities" or strangers, now I wasn't interested in receiving any opinion that wasn't recognition and amazement. I finally went to see the fresco. Only someone who has created something knows how that thing decomposes. As soon as I saw Jesus Christ, I knew that no hand foreign to art, or the hand of some painter's apprentice, or of some imbecile painter, had deformed what my brushes had given life to. The damage was minimal—maybe invisible to any other viewer—but implacable. The same thing happened with Judas, to a lesser degree than with Jesus Christ, but now I could speak of the traitor as "what remained of him." My anger and sadness, my solitude and sense of time poorly earned and poorly spent, made me flee from that scene, almost in slow-motion and with my hand raised—as if I were meditating on something and didn't want to be interrupted or to talk with anyone I happened to bump into—covering my eyes, which bitter tears sprang from. For me the work was finished because there was no way of repairing the mistake, of restoring the moment. Judas disintegrates because he no longer looks at Christ; the only Christ he was able to see. I chose badly. I trusted that Judas would show me something. He was looking at something but not at the supreme maker, the true deity. God presented his son one time ... and Judas, who could see him didn't do so . . . That supper was and wasn't in Jerusalem as much as in my fresco. And that's fair. At that moment Judas wasn't looking at Jesus. He didn't see him. The same thing happened to the other figures as happens to us men: they aged. That the process may have accelerated because of my rash and, finally, failed experiments is an argument that isn't completely false, but definitely exaggerated.

It's difficult to draw a portrait of the son of God. To paint the image of God incarnate. What surrounded me was always enough. Sound theology. I'd like to live another hundred years. Sound Christianity. It wasn't the King of France but indeed a prince who held me in his arms. I could complain about many things that have been said and written about my person, but doing that would make no sense: it's the luck that any human being runs. The only thing that Master Dante's Hell, Purgatory, and Paradise have in common is that the whole world complains about those who are still on Earth. The antagonism between the living and the dead predates anything else.

Charlottesville, November 13, 1998

Biographical Information

Roberto Ransom (b. 1960, Mexico City) is an award-winning narrative writer whose published work includes novels, short-story collections, poetry, and books of essays as well as children's literature. In addition to his *Desaparecidos, animales y artistas* (1999), his published work includes two other short-story collections, *Saludos a la familia* (1995), and *Vidas colapsadas* (2012); and the novels *En esa otra tierra* (1991), *La línea de agua* (1999), *Te guardaré la espalda* (2003), *Los días sin Bárbara* (2006) and *Permiso para ausentarse* (forthcoming). His *A Tale of Two Lions* was published by Norton in 2007. Ransom holds degrees from UNAM and the University of La Salle and also studied at the Colegio de México. He earned his Ph.D. from the University of Virginia, where as a Fulbright-Robles García scholar he wrote his dissertation on Graham Greene's works on Mexico. He holds tenure at the Autonomous University of Chihuahua (School of Fine Arts and School of Humanities). He lives in Chihuahua with his wife and three children.

Daniel Shapiro received a grant from the PEN Translation Fund and a fellowship from the National Endowment for the Arts to translate Roberto Ransom's *Desaparecidos, animales y artistas*. His translations, poems, and prose have appeared in *American Book Review*, *The American Poetry Review*, *BOMB*, *Brooklyn Rail*, *CNN.com*, and *The Oxford Book of Latin American Poetry*. His translation of *Cipango*, by Chilean poet Tomás Harris (2010), received a starred review in *Library Journal*. He is the author of the poetry collections *The Red Handkerchief and Other Poems* (2014) and *Woman at the Cusp of Twilight* (2016). Shapiro is Distinguished Lecturer and Editor of *Review: Literature and Arts of the Americas* at The City College of New York, CUNY.

Swan Isle Press is a not-for-profit publisher
of poetry, fiction, and nonfiction.

For information on books of related interest or
for a catalog of new publications contact:
www.swanislepress.com

Missing Persons, Animals, and Artists
Designed by Marianne Jankowski
Typeset in Adobe Jensen Pro
Printed on 55# Glatfelter Natural